KALDER

Head in the Clouds – Book 2

C.E. Wright

Knoxville, Tennessee
crippledbeaglepublishing.com

Cover art created by bobooks, https://www.fiverr.com/bobooks
Manuscript artwork and cover art design created by C.E. Wright

Follow on Twitter @CE_WRIGHT8

Paperback ISBN 978-1-958533-23-9, 978-1-958533-24-6
Hardcover ISBN 978-1-958533-22-2, 978-1-958533-25-3

Library of Congress Control Number: 2023902677

Printed in the United States of America

Praise for Petrichor,

Book 1 of the Head in the Clouds Series

"Overall a really enjoyable and quick read, and I think about
the characters pretty frequently in my day.
Also, a dragon book without humans? Win!"
—Daniel A., professional animator

"I think Hurricane is a great character and has a lot of
depth[…] Windshift is a great character, and when Hurricane
meets him is probably my favorite scene of the book[…] All
in all, very great story and I kept wanting
to read to see what happened."
—Matthew L.

"I'm excited to see more from this series! Would
recommend to Wyvern and Dragon lovers, a
new great fantasy series is taking flight!"
—User "coooooooool" on Amazon

"Petrichor is beautifully written. I went into it with high
hopes and was not disappointed. It made
me laugh, contemplate, and gave me one or two shocks.
Altogether a pleasant reading experience
and I look forward to more from Wright soon."
—Margaret S.

"I would not have expected such a short book to give so much[...] The social abuse by members
[of] the dominant priest caste, and a backstory forcing the [main character] Hurricane to earn her family's keep, are cause for many hardships she overcomes as she can, doing what she must, unfaltering.
And the progressive exposition delivers some good unexpected slaps and surprises."
—Pierre K.

To my mother, who soothed my fire when the ink from my pen couldn't fall.

Cama
Hendokia Range
Saeri Desert
Sœr
Yurie
Baisa Bay
Rojo
Middle Lakes
Alvoreçer Jungle
Ellora
Amer
Lowern
Capitole
Kinli
Alvoreçer
= Capital
= Kaozar's home
= Mountains
= Plains
= Volcanic plains

Faith is a fine invention
When Gentlemen can see—
But Microscopes are prudent
In an Emergency.
Emily Dickinson

Chapter I

HURRICANE

My wings want to die. I have never, *ever* flown this much. From what I've learned as a wyvern, being a winged creature means you must fly to live. Walking is for the weak. I am at peace with using my legs, but the air feels much, much better back through that portal. To take up time and to distract myself, I try to see what else is different in this world.

This universe has a sky, which means that they have flying animals, which also means that my wings don't give me the advantage I thought I would have. *Kaozaris have wings. In fact, wings are all the Kaozaris have other than their bodies attached to the wings. Windshift's book never specified if they have any camouflage powers. Kaozaris could be right next to me and attack, and I wouldn't know it. Even though I'm far away from the beach where I first heard that rustling noise, my heart still pounds at the thought of not being alone. If they were to attack, how would they do it?* I brace myself for agony. Nothing.

Well, there is nothing until an irregular wind pattern brushes past my cheek, and I yelp. *What was that?* Just a blackbird whizzes past me. Nothing but a bird. Who knew that birds exist here too? I consider him my only friend in this new place, but he squawks at my face and disappears into the clouds. I guess I will never see him again.

Water is everywhere I look. The expanse of ocean around me exemplifies how small I am, but the fathoms beckon me to the waves. I dip down and open my mouth to drink, but the saltiness makes me spit it out. I really need to stop forgetting that I have water in my canteen, but I need to ration it for 'future me's' sake. For now, I take in the scenery.

Sunset finally ripples within the endless, blue blanket of ocean. The vermilions and the oranges bathe the sky in pure gold. Who knew this dystopia could be beautiful? I swim in the clouds. I prefer not to swim in the ocean. The creatures may be in there. The drawings depict them with fins on the ends of their tails, so my theory is plausible. *They still have wings, Hurricane.* Not knowing the location of my enemies, I jolt away from the clouds. Even the clouds could be cruel. But they are safe. They have to be.

Islands dapple the deep azure under me. *Is this the continent? I can't grab my book right now to check the map, but I might have to land on one of the smaller islands. My wings will give out.* I land on the pink sand and lie down. *I made it.* While rubbing the soft, rosy sand between my talons, I gaze upon the setting sun on the horizon. *How come Windshift never created beaches? If he did, I would've stayed there forever, listening to the ebb and flow of the lapping waves and the leaves of the palm trees rustling. How come I've never experienced this before?* I lie in silence and, for the first time today, without fear. Noticing my talon prints in the sand, I realize that this is the one pair on this whole, desolate, perhaps abandoned beach. I frown. But that's all that will be until I find all the gods' vials, and I'll need to get used to the feeling of flying alone. The silence is driven out by the buzz of the insects behind the wall of trees in the jungle. I sigh, know the forest calls me, and enter its murk.

The humidity is disgusting. I spot a fruit tree, and because the growling in my stomach will call all the wild animals to me, I take a chance to relieve the noise. I sink my teeth into the fruit, and, according to my deductive reasoning, it's not poisonous. My cares are gone as I ravenously tear through bananas, papayas, and pears. *Hooray, they have a type of pears.*

With my stomach full, I feel less tempted to eat the fruit I am storing in my bag for tomorrow morning. Next, I need shelter, and the trees will protect me the most from predators. So, I go there first. Windshift must be helping me from Castle Hill when I discover a grand nest in the nook between the branches and the trunk. Despite its disheveled nature, I can move the twigs that stick out too far and nestle in a comfortable position. The thick black of the jungle invigorates anyone who lives here, especially the bugs and perhaps the predators. But I have to be safe, so wrapping myself with these leaves and vines seems like a good idea. Now that night has fallen, the temperature is more bearable, and this camouflage will keep me warm enough. *I wonder if the moon has risen back in Petrichor.* Then, I stop camouflaging and wonder if my family is safe. Somehow, I don't feel like securing myself anymore while they're waiting in Castle Hill for me after I lied to them. While lying on my back and staring at the kaleidoscope of the canopy above, I imagine being back in that royal bedroom where Dust Devil told us everything. *Is Mother going to help him? What about Stratus? What about* Father? I grab the book's satchel tightly. *They have to be proud of him.*

I pray that they are. I pray that Stratus keeps her promise to protect them. My eyelids become heavier, and every time they close, I see their faces. *I made it this far, and I will continue in their name.*

In the morning, I perk up and mentally trace my steps back to the beach. *Maybe since I'm on foreign soil, the book will tell me where to find the coast.* But before I can peruse the map, the scent of smoke enters my nostrils. *Smoke, fire, Kaozaris? Are there some* here? While following the smell, I find a pathway through the thick, immutable forest. An indistinguishable voice can be heard half a league away down said path. Venturing around this new world will give me insight into my enemies. And it won't hurt to explore, I hope.

After discovering a shack at the end of the trail, I find many similar shacks clustered around it. Words of a chirping language and smoke both drift from the house's chimneys. I feel anticipation—a horrible feeling now—about the first interactions I will have with this new world. They will see me as an outsider. *They didn't see me last night, however. What should I do?* I think back to the art of the Kaozaris and figure that trying to look like them will help the most. For their featherless wings, I need my feathered ones to look as flat as theirs. So, using some mud, I paste thick palm leaves on the dorsal and ventral sides. *Gross.* For the color of my scales, I plaster on the mud wherever I can reach. *Also gross.* Now, what I need to do for those long black stripes on their faces is procure a dark substance. Snatching a pile of ash by an extinguished fire pit and accenting my face, I decide now I am ready.

I hop along the road and, at the sight of my first passerby, smile. An initial thought is that he looks nothing like the pictures. He walks on four legs (so apparently, they have legs), but I cannot see his finned tail. He pulls a wagon around his neck and over his body, the latter of which shines red in the sun. The stranger looks as if a warmly colored salamander decided to grow forearms and the ears of a small cat. Before I can leave, I catch him looking me up and down, narrowing his eyes, and proceeding to harrumph. Then he walks away, his wagon rattling with the sound of wooden tools.

Did he already know that I'm not a Kaozari? Did I fail that quickly? I run over to a puddle to check my reflection, and I am adequately covered. *At least he didn't say anything. Maybe I shouldn't smile next time I see someone.*

I march past the rest of the creatures, but now I have a grimace on my face. Either my face or simply their impoliteness makes the inhabitants quiet and focused on their own duties. The density of this market increases as I move along the streets, and fragrant bulbs of various tropical flora line the stalls' rooftops. *Not as busy and cluttered as Castle Hill*, I wonder, *but the activity in the market is still loud.*

My ears prick at the sound of a word I recognize—*food. Huh.* They talk in *my* language, but their voices sound like they come through a fan's filter. Stratus showed me this mechanical fan once, and I put my face right in front of the wind while talking to her (because who wouldn't stare at super-fast blades and not be totally mesmerized?). Somehow from that, my voice was altered. The voices here are like that, but they don't sound like nightmarish spirits.

I glance up at the gibberish signs and realize I have to learn some of the written language if I want to successfully invade.

"Oi." One of the voices in the crowd, not belonging to the language I can quasi-understand, perks up by my head. I jump back and whirl around in every direction to find the voice's owner.

"Oi." The voice belongs to a vendor, coated in feathers with a round face and a sharp beak. But she neither has horns nor any defining characteristics of a Kaozari. Windshift never told me of a creature like *this*. In her talons sits a small pastry basted in a shiny sauce. My mouth waters as she nudges it to me.

Should I take the pastry? If Windshift didn't tell me about creatures like her, maybe she's safe. She looks at me directly, expecting any response. "Well, do you have samples?" I pray for my question to translate correctly.

She narrows her eyes and turns her head. "Hm?"

Let me try again. "Samples?" I ask, gesturing to the food. She still stares at me. "Try? Small?" I glance around at the other stalls to see what I'm doing wrong. A customer drops some flat coins in the talons of the vendor, and I, hoping that Windshift prepared me enough, jingle my bag for the sound of currency. *Of course he did.*

After handing her a coin, she gives me the pastry and some change. *She does not question the lack of fire on my spine, but she still looks at me like I'm a foreigner. Technically, I am.* Maybe she'll stop looking at me if I eat. So, I shove the entire thing into my mouth and chew, looking down at the dusty dirt ground and feeling ashamed of my gluttony. Considering that this doesn't have enough sugar to destroy my teeth, I am more able to enjoy the berries and crisp pastry shell.

I nod. "Thank you."

The bird lady smiles, thinks, and picks another dessert from her display. Then, she offers it to me. I have no issue with paying her for another taste, but when I reach into my bag, she shakes her head. I take a moment to register the smile on her beak. *She's giving me a gift.*

So far, the two creatures I've met haven't been too bloodthirsty. In fact, they're not bloodthirsty at all. Most of all, I appreciate this vendor's kindness. No evil cretin would ever create such a lovely confection like this and then give me another one for free.

Then the spice hits. "Oh, no. Oh, no, no." Everything hurts, and I can't even cough because the spice feels like it's burning my throat. I know this is not poison because I have felt this spice before (*curse you Stratus*) and have not died. But I need to get this out of me.

She tries to calm me down with words I cannot understand as I try to find my canteen. I recognize the end of a question: "Better?" I shake my head as I rub my neck. *This isn't working.* I frantically find the canteen and guzzle it down. Finally, I can rest. When I smile with relief at the vendor, I stop and see fear flood her expression. Her eyes are wide, and her jaw is nearly on the counter.

I inspect my talons where a mass of mud and dirt that used to be on my neck sticks. Scales, not thick dust, are rough against my feathers. All this grime was for nothing.

The vendor shrieks to the feathered creatures behind the blocky carts. Then, she faces me. She clamps her front talons on the counter and heaves herself up, extending her sooty wings. A snarl escapes the depths of her throat. I've made that expression before and know it well; she hurls curses at me. Then, catching me off guard, the bird lady *tackles* me. Her talons grip around my throat. Through all this fury, I have no choice but to kick her off with my hind legs. She flies into several carts pulled by some of the pedestrians and she crashes.

Am I that strong?

The fellow merchants—both of the bird creatures and Kaozaris—face me and snarl, their white spears of teeth stained with fuchsia. I run as fast as I can, dipping between the shoppers who either have no idea or every idea about what happened. I do not look back, but I hear bellows tear through the air.

I make it to the thick of the jungle. The chirping of the insects and macaws cannot deafen any screams the bird creatures might let out. Desperate for a reprieve, I exhale a deep breath and slink along the branches. My wings are too big to fly here; they would be axes against the limbs.

The roaring returns. I hide up in the canopy to see the vendor and three other birds scour the forest floor. The other three birds wear glistening wooden armor, but the mud still on my scales will protect me better amongst these branches.

"Oko ra lo," one of them grumbles.

"Eilo ra lo ave al ruoz," the bird lady snaps, tasting the air. They search below for a few minutes as I try to ponder my next move. I can either stay here until the end of time with my heart racing and shallow breathing and pray they give up, or I can fly now and risk them hearing me. Well, it would not be a

risk. They would certainly hear me. I didn't look at the book before I went to the market, so I have absolutely no idea where I'm going and what I'm doing. The light ekes out from the canopy, and I estimate that the sun is east as of now. Since I came from the west, I can go in the opposite direction. With no other options, I zoom across the limb, and my speed causes my talon to wrest a branch completely off the trunk with an enormous cracking sound. Their heads whip up. *Great.*

As I dodge branches, I doubt they will ever stop chasing me. What I do know is that I can no longer stay here at the risk of dying. I also know that Windshift did not lie about these tricksters and savages. Windshift never lies.

After making it through the leaves, I land at the water's edge. The turquoise ocean sparkles, charming me to fly out to the sea. Beached, wooden structures scatter across the pink sand.

From a distance, the vendor cries, *"Marakoz. Oena nurait oko ei rana!"*

I don't have enough time to fly away. They'll easily cast magic and shoot me down.

For now, I search around the beach, worrying out loud at the pitch of a tea kettle and praying for Windshift's guidance. I run into an upside-down vessel and stub my toe. I screech at my toe for being so foolish as to run into this contraption and for making a sound. But I stop and realize the echo from within. I know this island was a trap, but *this* is a blessing, After gaming the size of the structure, I push it onto the water. Then, I swipe the sand with my tails to cover my tracks. The wood groans as the vessel sinks in the shallow depth. I crawl underneath, submerging myself in the water, and keep my nostrils, eyes, and ears above water.

"Oko? Oko?"

The hunting creatures stomp around, overturning the rest of the contraptions and dragging their tails through the sand. Finally, I have tricked the tricksters. I have won this feat. But other possibilities exist in this new world. I slide underneath the vessel, extend my wings, and burst out of the water. What mud I wore is now gone. My self-righteous laughter rings through the air. The growling vendor is about to follow me and possibly cut my throat, but one of the guards stops her with his tail and gestures to the water.

Why did they stop? What I do know is that I have tested Windshift's warning. Even though I have questioned him (I will not deny that), I know he is right. I need to be more careful. I need to be the savior I'm meant to be. For the rest of the day, I fly toward the new horizon.

Chapter II

I have changed my mind. This is a *curse*. This is a terrible trial Windshift has decided to put me through. He has led me into this heat, this horrible, scale-blistering heat, because of my family and how we have misinterpreted the nature of survival. It is not our fault. I insult myself for rehashing this fact again since I have nothing else to do. The important thing is that I keep my mind on my mistakes and confusion to distract myself from this heat because, my *goodness*, my scales might as well melt!

Finally, I arrive at the eastern shore of the continent. The craggy coast guarded by sentinel towers invites me downward, but I stay in the clouds to sneak up on the unsuspecting savages. Several feathered guards swarm the coast on the rocky, unpredictable beaches dotted with more of those buoyant, wooden structures. I lower through the clouds and slip by the marching armies without them noticing. Then, I check the ashy and charcoal ground. There must be Kaozaris here. *Excellent.* I can stand the temperature for now, but I do not know for how much longer. My turquoise scales stick out like a thorn.

I fly over an isolated, black plain, hardened and glowing with orange splotches where pale yellow patches of grass still give it life. The blades are translucent and wave softly in the breeze. I exhale as the peaceful wind caresses my face. The plain feels like a separate planet to me, being far underneath my talons, yet I can see every individual blade of grass.

Fearing that the bottoms of my feet will get burned, I soar down and float above the ground. I'll need my talons to attack. It does not look like there are more creatures here where I have arrived, so that might mean that I have skipped where the vial might be hidden. Wait, where *have* I landed? I rest on a patch of grass and open the satchel.

In the book, I locate the western archipelago of Alvoreçer that I passed through. On the map, the archipelago is colored dark green and unimportant, but I find the island I was just on and never will go on again: Kinli. I shrug and put the book back. I pop open the canteen and position it over my mouth to realize that I am completely and utterly out of water. I hiss at 'past me' for being too insatiable for her own good. Still, the oppressive heat smothers me, and I would be embarrassed if I died from dehydration instead of in battle against the Kaozaris.

The never-ending horizon taunts me as I plow my way through the desert in search of water. Nothing but dry grass and the occasional tree and maybe a mountain or two in the distance keep me company as I fly. I think I'm hallucinating when I notice the dark blue of a river down below. But the odor is foul. I land and investigate. Thick bushes with juicy, olive-green leaves block my view, so I hack through them and find the slowly flowing liquid, highlights of gold swirling about. I joyously cry and am about to bathe, but right before I submerge myself, I pause.

That's not water. That's way too thick and hot to be water. My paranoia is beginning to annoy me, but I got tackled yesterday. I have to be careful. Deceit is everywhere. I look back and forth to the ends of the river to see any incoming vessels. They have enticed me, so it only makes sense for them to take advantage of my interest in them and sneak up on me while I admire something I lack. None are in view, so I let out a breath. *I think I am fine. I do not know if I'm fine. They would not poison everything. They must be cleverer than that. Windshift said they were cleverer than that. They need to tantalize me.*

A roar behind me sounds off. I look behind and see eyes glaring from the bushes.

I catch myself saying, "Wait … "

A thick, russet beast slithers out of the bush. Needle claws and stocky legs pop out of the beast's torso.

"Wait–"

The beast charges. I immediately jump over the water, but as I flap my wings, the beast's jaw clamps on my thigh. I try knocking it off with my talons, but I cannot reach that far.

Instead, I scream. My cries do not appear to work.

I clumsily flap a good distance away from the river and flail around in the sky with the beast dangling from my leg. But the beast's teeth are deep in my scales and threatening to pull me down. The horizon blurs completely with my dehydration, blood loss, and screeches.

A bark from the sky rumbles through the air, and a dot of red flies toward me. Registering it isn't just flying toward me but rather *bolting*, I prepare for magic. Outside of training at Castle Hill, I have never cast lightning as a defense from creatures I had not predicted the existence of back in Petrichor, even though I always wanted to use it against Tornado. So, now that I see what I assume is a Kaozari I know and have studied the attacks of, I feel confident enough to let loose my magic. I have no choice after all. Sparks gather in my jaws.

It narrowly avoids my lash of lightning and tackles the beast on my thigh. The dash of red knocks the air out of me and makes my head spin with its sheer speed.

The creature also looks nothing like the drawings. Even though youthful, dark red scales dazzle its body, it has a *furred* neck and tail. What strikes me the most is the excessive fabric stretching from the knees to the collarbone.

That fabric gets covered with spit and dark blood as it slashes the beast and slams it into the ground with a clap of energy and a sizzle of heat. Dust floats to where we are in the sky as it looks at me for the first time.

"*Za rlaçi ol muk repi?*" He asks.

"Where is it?"

The electricity threatens to shoot at him before his eyes widen. He stares at me, flapping his slender wings in the air. "*Puro klaçia ra?*"

I clench my teeth to avoid falling out of consciousness but in vain.

The last things I see before darkness are his eyes; the right is azure, and the left is honey gold.

Chapter III

What I can see of the stars embedded in the indigo sky gives no light to the arid desert ahead of me. Even if the soft light were to shine, the cave I'm in would block it out. *Why am I in a cave?* I force open my eyes and take a look around.

The cave's russet walls are barren. Next to my talons is a wooden bowl, painted with images of orange lilies and filled with transparent liquid. Even though the small fire to my left is ablaze, the shadow of whatever is on the other side covers me. My eyes adjust and recognize the face of my savior. I jolt and wince at my leg's wounds. He hushes me. I do not know why I or this creature are here. All I know is that I am not here by accident. I also know that this is my third challenge. First through the birds, second through the heat, and third through the dark quiet of negotiation.

He inhales deeply and lets out the breath, its warmth creating steam that billows and condensates on my scales. "You're one of them."

His Petrichorish is impeccable.

My feathers bristle. "One of who?"

He murmurs to himself indiscernibly. He rubs his temples and scrunches up his nose. *He is distracted.* I can run now. Then, he pauses as some sort of realization dawns on his face. "What is your name?"

I look at my wound, bound by some navy strip to stop the bleeding. Then I look back at him. I study his face, which tells me of his intent, curiosity, and innocence. Then, I hear another voice in my head, and I say, "Violet."

He narrows his eyes. "That can't be true. You wyverns don't use that naming system."

"I'm not lying. My name is Violet."

I imagine the map of this continent in my head. "I come from the mountains." The map makes me think of the book. I inconspicuously reach for my neck, and the book is safe and sound in the satchel. "Yes, I come from the northern mountains."

"No. You don't." He dusts off the two black lines that lead from his burning eyes to his beak. "You are a wyvern from Petrichor."

I chuckle. "Wyvern? Such a strange word."

"Windshift is real, isn't he?" He knows the name of my god. Back beyond that portal, Windshift never told me if they knew of my existence. But this creature knows more than what he lets on. I try to speak, but I cough. "Shh," he says, raising his talons as if trying to calm a wild animal. "When you were being attacked by that crocodile, you fell unconscious, and I took you to this cave where you would be safe."

"That beast is called a crocodile?"

"You won't have to worry about it anymore." He pats the cloth bag to his left. I gulp. He asks, "Do you have them in your world?"

His interrogation reminds me to keep on the defensive. That means to me that I keep quiet.

"Do you mind telling me what you meant?" He asks. "When you asked me where 'it' was?"

I bite my cheek. Tornado's wound has mostly healed, but I have other pain to focus on.

He leans back, inhaling deeply. "Who *are* you really?"

"I have more of a right to ask who you are." I start to rise, wincing at my leg's pain but covering it up with a conniving snarl. I manifest the spirit of an annoying ferret with terrible dehydration.

"I'm Sparik. I work for Kaozar and was sent for the crocodile, but then I found you." He wraps his navy cloak with a missing strip closer to his body. "Have you ever noticed that it gets cold at night in the desert? And not your ordinary cold either. Did Windshift create deserts for you?" His voice quietens. "Kaozar did for us–"

"Sparik, are you going to hurt me?"

"Relax, Violet–"

"Aha!" Widening my wings, I stand. "Ow. You thought my name was Violet? I just looked up at the sky, and it kinda looked purple, so I thought that would be a good name to disguise myself. Completely impromptu. My name is Hurricane."

"Relax … Hurricane." I drift down but still keep my posture aggressive to hide my surprise. He bares his pale palms possibly to show he is not a threat. "So, I have an idea for why you are here." He leans forward, and the fire lights up his face's spikes. He points at me. "You were sent by Windshift to retrieve all the vials." My heart drops. "From Kaozar, Giddrath, and Surrveseig. Then you return with the magic, and it sets him free."

I ball my talons into fists but keep my expression flat.

I have two pathways. I lie and somehow escape this "Sparik" and continue on my quest alone. Whatever he does is out of my control. My name will be known in the streets as a danger to this society. My cover is blown, yes, but my plan is not.

Pathway two encourages more risk. To understand it, I take pathway one into consideration. Yes, I may escape. I am smaller than Sparik so I can maneuver through his attacks easily. But I have no water or food once I'm gone. My leg is injured too, and whatever is out there is definitively worse than the warmth of the fire and the bowl of painted orange lilies next to me. Even though my safety is in question here, the stars won't shine on me.

"Yes." I'll play his game.

"Ah, I see." He props his head on his talons. "Are you a servant of his? Perhaps from the castle?"

"Why are you asking me this? You already know everything." I didn't want this lowly stranger to know all my secrets. Then again, he knows very little about me. *How does he know about the vials? And why did he save me?*

"I'm curious. I'm just wondering … Why you?"

I lumber up and spread my wings to their full span. The fire laps and snarls around me. "I was chosen by him. I have every right to be here, to prove myself. I will save my kind from you sinners."

"Prove yourself?"

"I was chosen!"

"Hurricane. I know how you feel."

"So you think you can save me but then keep me away from the one thing I need–"

"Hurricane, I hate him."

"Who?"

"*Kaozar.*"

I freeze. While I slink down behind the fire, Sparik stands on his back two feet and clasps his talons in front of him. Windshift never told me of these creatures posing like this. "I have worked with my god for as long as I have lived. Ever since I hatched, I was reared in the ways of the castle, in his ways. But since I opened my eyes, he saw me as his little worker ant. A puppet. He does nothing as all of his servants slave for him." He hangs his head. "And every day when I pass by the vial, I see my reflection. It's humiliating." He slumps.

Out of all of the deities' creatures, I meet the one with an independent mind. It's also a malleable mind. But does it need to be molded by me? *He saved me. He saw the turquoise of my scales, knew I was "one of them," and saved me, nevertheless.* I sniff the water to my left.

"I bought that from a nearby trader," he says. "You can have it or not. I understand that you may not trust me. I have no clue what Windshift told you about us. But if you want to survive here, you're going to have to be hydrated."

The dust in my mouth builds with the realization that the life in me needs that water. I haven't been poisoned thus far (the spice doesn't count). Sparik could've let me get killed. But I'm intact. Dilapidated but still breathing. If I want to keep on breathing, I might start trusting him. I stick my tongue in it.

"Does it taste good?" In confirmation, I chug the whole thing. "I take that as a yes."

My throat is at peace. I sigh. "I'm sorry that Kaozar treats you like that."

"You're the first … anyone to tell me that."

"I understand. Where I'm from, I'm a puppet too. I have to behave a certain way in order to be able to live."

"A certain way?"

"I can't tell you what I have to do. But I'm a servant too along with helping my family. The only reason I'm not dead yet is because I support them by hunting." I lean forward, careful not to let the fire pit singe my unkempt fur spine. "Why did you save me?"

"It was the right thing to do. I won't let another creature that passes through this continent be harmed by whatever my god has created."

His words make sense of the lack of poison in my stomach. "We're more alike than I thought."

"It sounds that way."

The dying fire crackles between us. The sweat congeals into my scales.

He smooths out the spiked, short fur around his neck. "I have an idea." He swirls one talon over the fire, and its flames follow and disappear into the air one by one. Sparik balances an ember on the tip of his claw. Then, he evaporates it. "I can help you get the vial."

Jaw slacked, I jump at him. "Huh?"

He scrabbles back. "While you were unconscious, I was thinking of a plan. It requires both you and I to make it work. And it'll be risky, but it's worth it. For the vial. Will you be willing to listen to me?"

I pause, rubbing the sticky air off my eyes' spikes. Then I guffaw, my voice echoing through the cave. "You're kidding. You have to be kidding me."

He tilts his head. "Why would I 'kid' you?"

I scoff. "And why should I trust you?"

"It's in the cistern in Capitole. In the middle of the lava pit, it lies on a brick pedestal created by gold cement. Only the authorized can touch it." On the ground, he gathers a pile of dirt and, with his talon, scratches a diagram of exactly what he described.

I freeze. Kaozar would be even more of a fool not to keep his vial with him. But I have to be aware of the specificity of his claims. They're so peculiar. I sigh. So, they have to be true. The shadows flickering on the cave walls blur with the recognition that the vial *is near*.

"When I first saw you, you almost died. You're in danger here." He exhales as his fire gently cascades from the tip of his nose to the tip of his tail. "Just hear me out."

"Windshift told me–"

"Not to trust us? Yes, I know, I know. But listen to this. I disguise you like a Kaozari plebe trying to talk to Kaozar himself. Maybe to request a blessing. I have to drop off this meat for him, so you will meet him eventually. Then once we're alone, we go into the vial's room before dawn. Then we escape. If we find guards, we can fight them. We stay under the radar, and we get one step closer to ridding ourselves from the forces that control us. What do you say?"

I inspect him. The black splotches on his thin, angular face remind me of a large predatory cat. But this little mouse of vermin has pupils the size of raisins. I enable a deliberate silence in order to listen to any pleas for taking everything he said back. So far, I hear nothing. I have to ask. "What kind of death wish does your species have?"

"Do you want the honest answer or the diplomatic one?"

"The former."

"We have one of a kind."

The plan is finally laid in front of me. I don't even have to worry about working out the details. A like-minded individual and I will carry the magic that, with one drop, can conquer this continent. Windshift will be pleased. But he won't be pleased if I never return. If I die, I'll have myself to blame. Then my family will have to hear the news. Father will cry and so will Mother. But I imagine Dust Devil the most. By Windshift's torrents, the look on their faces will never compare to his. He'll be trapped in that house *and* his body. Back at the house, he'll be trapped with only Mother until he turns twenty. The worst part is that, maybe, they'll never even know I'm dead. I've come too close to failure now. I'm not ready. I don't want to taste the bitter viscera of death.

"I'm sorry. I'm so sorry, but this is too much. I can't do this plan. And I don't want to meet Kaozar."

He pauses and sighs. "Understood, Hurricane."

"I've been through enough. I don't want to go in this quickly just yet. It's too much. Too risky. I have a family back at home, Sparik. If I'm going to die, I want them to be by my side."

"I totally understand. It's your journey." He gets up again. "Can I get you anything?"

I trace the edge of the wooden bowl. "I'd hate to ask you for anything else."

"It's the least I can do."

I nudge the bowl toward his nearly white talons. "Can I have some more water please?"

"Of course." He takes up the bowl and goes to a corner of the cave. He pours what is left from a cowhide bottle in his bag into the bowl. The transparent water gurgles out of the leather container.

I figure that I have avoided a truly grave mistake, so I have reason to figure out more about this world. "Can I ask you a question, Sparik?"

"Of course."

"Why was that water by the river dark and thick, but that water you're pouring out clear? Like the water in Petrichor?"

"Oh." He caps the bottle. "Because that wasn't water you saw back there. That was lava."

"What's lava?"

"Here, I can show you. Look outside." Getting up gingerly, I follow his gaze and scour the desolate, dark sand from the cave. "Do you see the smoke to the left of that big rock?"

"Yes."

"That's coming from a small lava spring."

"Must be scorching hot water."

"It's melted rock. If you touch that, your scales will burn."

"Oh, no. How come you all have it everywhere? Why is there a whole river of it?"

"Kaozaris drink and swim in lava," Sparik says. "Our bodies are built for it, and we enchant our wood so the docks and any transportation we use won't sizzle up in the canals. You won't find any water here. Oh, speaking of which." My ears prick at the sound of him placing the bowl next to me.

My face falls in horror. "So, when I leave, I'll die of thirst?"

"Oh, no. There are convertors for the other species who visit for business. You'll find a common use one on the side of the road, but it's not free. Maybe Windshift gave you some maktae to spend." He smiles and folds his thin wings, showing the crimson dorsal side. "You're free to stay for the night. I'll stay by you for protection, and you can ask whatever you want about this world. I'm an open book." I think I catch him glancing at my satchel. "And then you can leave in the morning." His face tells me that I am an anomaly: something to be afraid of but also to respect.

I nod, drink the water, and sigh.

While Sparik unfolds a blanket to lie on, I gaze at the stars. Maybe they can put me to sleep. They start to shine now. Then they start to blur. My head spins. Then my vision goes dark a little too quickly for comfort.

Chapter IV

Rough, tight burlap blocks any light from entering my eyes. After my blindfold is ripped off my face, I notice Sparik, cloaked in dark blue. I must have slept well. But I do not remember burlap from last night. I take a glance around, and I learn that I am the most careless wyvern in the world.

The floating structure I am trapped in creaks gradually through lava. I thrash around, but Sparik presses his tail on my body. I screech loudly and toward anyone in the sandstone buildings along this river. He tightens the binds around my mouth and keeps paddling. The lengths of his strength are unknown to me.

Sparik leads me to the dock of a wider section of the river. Polished, brown vessels, some with lion figureheads, dot the deadly water, each with enough room for two and some cargo. He reaches below and grabs a long, pale paddle with carvings of waves and jutting rocks.

I have the opportunity to summon magic and destroy him, but I don't want to fall into the lava. I wheeze and attempt to speak despite the metal binding around my mouth. "Hey."

"What?"

"Hew der you? Ye *drugged* me!"

He pauses to consider this. "I recommend you keep your volume low. It will make this a lot easier." Vessels carrying heaping sacks of wheat navigate alongside us.

I recognize the Bird Lady's species, with their large golden fur manes and sharp beaks.

"Sparik, Sparik," I hiss.

He loosens my binding enough so I can speak clearly. "Hm?"

"Did you seriously think this would work? Capturing me and bringing me to my death?"

He narrows his eyes and squats to meet my glare. He scrutinizes my face for a while as I heave what breaths can escape from my lungs and whispers, "Say another word and you're dead."

"Help! Help–" He places down the oar and whips out a silver dagger. He holds it to my throat. The fire rages now, but his thousand league stare burns brighter. I try to wince, but I physically can't. Instead, my throat feels the aftermath of dehydration and my cries for help. Sparik slips the dagger back in its sheath, tightens my binding again, and continues paddling.

We are now a measly dot in the mass of structures. As my metal clinks on the wooden floor of the vessel, I shift in a more comfortable position (or rather as comfortable as I can be right now) and examine my surroundings. Even if my wings weren't bound, there would be no great chance of escape. A new bridge passes over my head every minute, and the merchants glance in my direction. I try to shoot some sparks out of my nose to get their attention.

"Now, I have questions for you," he says. Immediately, I dip my head back down, knowing I should be more subtle. Plus, I'm not in Petrichor. I'm bound to the back of a weird floating structure and being taken to who knows where. No one's going to help me. "Many questions, in fact. As long as you don't try to kill me with that lightning gathering in your mouth right now, this will be easy." My teeth are clenched so tight that I didn't notice my power surging. "I'll loosen up the clamp. *Don't try anything.*"

I'm smart enough not to make the same mistake again. I don't want my second punishment to be worse. *Do I lie? Or do I show pride for my own kind?* He loosens the binding.

"What are you *doing*? What is going through that leather-head's mind?" he asks, still navigating us. "Your Windshift, I mean."

I will ignore the insult, but I will neither forgive nor forget. "He shepherds us all with the grace of an eagle and with a flick of his talons. He is grander than you spineless whelps would ever be. He—" Sparik's fire grows as smoke sifts from his nostrils.

"This is not the time to spew propaganda." That phrase is said softly but barbed with thorns.

I peek and see Capitole's mouth, as described briefly in the book. *The book!* My heart drops at the realization that the satchel is missing from around my neck.

"Are you missing something?" He smirks.

How am I going to get it back? Who is he? What's going to happen to me? If I lose the book, I'm done for, and so is my kind's entire existence. If these binds were gone, the only thing left of him would be his ashes.

What I do know of Capitole is mainly about the canal which splits the city in half. Orange paper lanterns sway from cobblestone bridges over the lava. Flying Kaozaris and Bird Lady clones swarm the sky, but the majority of the inhabitants are by the stalls, on the bridges, or splashing in the shallow end of the lava. The scent of energy in the air is familiar. Deadly. "Continue, but do not dare make your voice louder than mine," he says. "Is he how the books describe him? Windshift?"

"Four wings, horns like mine. Black fur, green, six eyes. *Magnificent.*"

"Kaozar told me the truth, then." He paddles. "What's your living situation?"

"None of your business."

An hour of silence passes. The loose binding is still too tight for me, and the heat from the lava beneath me drips sweat down into my eyes. But I can't move, so I have to let it slide down. *And how are they used to this stench? Living by this river must be awful. What do I do?* My heart pounds. *Windshift, give me strength.* So, I tell him, "I work with my family and serve Windshift."

"I can't hear you."

"Don't make me repeat it," I say, thrashing.

He holds me down. "What does he tell you about *us*? The dragons and griffins."

Dragons and griffins ... that's what they're called. "He told me that you stole his magic and locked him and us away on our continent. Your dragons and griffins didn't bat an eye, and I'm here for revenge." No response. "Should I speak louder now?"

He bends down and faces me, still paddling and somehow going perfectly straight. *Does he have eyes on the back of his head?* "I hate to interrupt this, but I have an errand to run. You are going to stay here. Then, I will get us out of here, and then we can converse more about our cultural pleasantries. Well, in this case, we'll just talk about you because …" He chuckles in disbelief and merges to the left of the river.

The vessel creaks to a stop by one of the docks in between the tall buildings instead of the narrow boardwalk. Sparik steps out and taps shiny buttons on a silver box on top of a pole. "We'll be here for about thirty minutes. Stay on the boat, and don't talk to anyone."

I nod for now.

"I want verbal confirmation that you will stay on the boat."

"Yes, fine, I will stay on the boat." *Boat, not vessel.*

He pauses, clamps me tightly, and secures my bondage. "Good. I will return with some water. Kaozar will want you alive. Most likely." Then he closes burlap on my head. I close my eyes and try to think, but I'm distracted by listening to the staccato of the Kaozari's vivacious language. It's the same one I heard back on the island, which means I can understand most of what is spoken, but the various accents hamper my comprehension.

I need a new plan. The first action item is never to trust anyone ever again. I need to exorcise my foolishness. How I will do that is through redemption.

To start, I need to plan my escape. If words mean nothing to Sparik, they mean nothing to me. He's the one who gave me time to fly away after all by leaving me here. I shall bite through the metal around my snout, use my magic against the clamps to break them, and take flight, not without snatching my map. The vendors here won't do anything. I'm sure I fly better than them.

Next, I'll go to the coast to drink the water from the ocean. Even though it's salty and gross, I will be kept alive. Then I can go along the coast and get the vial myself. *But I can't just dart back and forth from the volcano to the ocean. That's too complicated. Also, the risk that Sparik will see me again is too great. Who am I kidding? I can't leave, but I can't stay.*

The boat shakes. Peppery language screams in my ear. *"Rela, puro ra?"* I freeze.

Then whoever is on this boat shakes me. Warm talons pat around my covered body, and the stranger mutters to himself. My sight slowly becomes restored when he pulls back my burlap. Now, I'll provide Sparik's comeuppance.

I flail around in the boat and glower at the intruder. I snarl at him before I realize that this dragon stands and has red scales like Sparik, but he does not have heterochromia.

"Remove yourself!" The actual Sparik marches over to the edge of the dock while carrying a bucket of sloshing water. He gingerly places the bucket down to his side.

The stranger gasps and leaps out of the boat. Sparik's face droops, and he pulls his hood tighter over his face. *Why would he have this reaction to being recognized?* Then, his head to the ground, the stranger falls to his knees and bows on the dock by Sparik's talons.

"O Mayi Sparik. My greatest, most profound apologies." He slaps his forehead. "I trespassed on his son's property. How could I be so foolish? Please forgive me, Your Grace."

His son? Sparik clenches his teeth. He glances from my confounded expression back to the reverent stranger. Then he notices that this stranger's praise piques the interest of the merchants. He closes his eyes and takes a deep breath. "You are forgiven. Please be pardoned and return from whence you came."

"You're a savior. I and the rest of your followers will be by your talons every step when you rule Kalder by Kaozar's side. We're here for you. I bid you well." His wings quiver, and he bows again before scrambling away into the mass of creatures spying on this spectacle. Sparik just stands there, basking in the veneration fed to him. *Why does he deserve praise like that? Who* is *he?*

"You spineless rat!" someone from the crowd screams. A dragoness steps in and spreads her wings. "I've been requesting your council for *three weeks,* but your staff dismisses me every single time. You think *you* can rule Kalder? Whoever supports you is mindless."

Half of the crowd decries her, and the other half is reticent in anticipation. Sparik eyes me and darts his focus away. "Everyone, everyone, silence. I have official business in the volcano now. Please, I command you to return to your duties. Bless you all." He hops in the boat and grabs a cloak to cover me. This time he rips open a hole and loosens my binding again, setting the water in front of me.

When the taut fabric covers my eyes, I can still imagine the expressions of the passerby. All of them gawked at Sparik, similar to how I admire Windshift. But I hear an uproar in the crowd alongside the canal. These cheers and denouncements thrown at Sparik make me realize I may have severely misjudged the power of this strange, lying Kaozari who also threatened to kill me. *Well,* I think, meandering down the isolated street of unconsciousness yet again, *he won't get to me as long as I get to him first.*

Chapter V

Thud. The boat's figurehead bumps into the dock. Once I realize the sack is off my head, I take a breath. The smells of basalt and steam, instead of clean air, are around me, and I cough.

Sparik prods my wings. "We've arrived. Out." He unbinds my legs, and I try to slash him with my talons. But because I have not walked in at least a day, I stumble over, rocking the boat. Lava splashes on my left wing, and once I start yelping, he opens a bottle of pink ointment. As he begrudgingly rubs the medicine between my feathers, he dabs some of it under his tongue. Sparik helps me regain my balance as I hobble out of the boat onto the dock. Green succulents sprawl from the woodwork supporting us. He tells me to keep close. *I have no other choice.*

He ties the boat onto the dock, hands five square coins to a soldier, weighed down by the metal plates around his chest and arms, and curtly nods to him. The worker bows, his dark red cape hanging down like a pendulum in the wind. Sparik tells me to be silent as we rush down the cobblestone streets. Touching each rock is like grabbing on for dear life to the one lukewarm thing on this land. I take it as comfort–the only comfort I have as I am rendered flightless with the binds on my wings. I pause to realize my powerlessness, and he grabs my neck and forces me down the streets.

We maneuver around swooping, tan buildings with fog slithering down the brick-colored shingles. More dragons and griffins exit their houses to pour lava into their tropical plants and grab the little papers posted on their patios.

Sparik leads me to a booth where he purchases two pieces of thick, foreign paper. He leads me down a dark alley, and we emerge beside another river, this one with a deeper amber glow underneath the currents. We stop by a booth, and Sparik hands the two pieces of paper to the griffin worker. He smiles gratefully at Sparik and leads us to an open metal box in the middle of the river with a ledge beside it. Escorting us across the small bridge leading to the mysterious contraption, he closes us inside. Before I touch the metal around me, I want Sparik to know I'm not stupid; ergo, I sit on my cloak instead of the steaming hot box. I can't attack here. This is his environment. Sparik's scales aren't burning from the walls. He takes off his hood and hands me a flask. I watch it steadily.

"Drink it."

"How do I know you didn't drug this one?"

"Well, if you die from poison, it's better than dying from a heat stroke. Many of my prisoners told me on their deathbeds that the former is quicker and less painful."

I grab the drink with my available, stubby talons on my wings and finish it in two seconds.

"And I was *hoping* that you would nurse that one for a bit."

I pout out of spite. "*Oops.*" He puts his talons on the brass lion head sticking out of a long, leather sheath. Understanding immediately, I bow my head and nudge the bottle to his feet.

The funicular awakens and lunges forward. I jolt from the sudden movement.

I say, "Just know that if this box wasn't here right now, you'd be dead."

Completely ignoring me, he says, "Don't be alarmed by the funiculars. They're very private." He knocks on the wall. "And also thick. They move us up and down the volcano when we don't want to fly." He walks past me and slides open the window.

The end of the lava river slinks up a gigantic mountain. Charred lava pools downward from the craggy opening at the top. I look behind us, and identical funiculars follow us with the same speed and equal distance between them. Before they can see my turquoise scales, I slide back in and close the window promptly.

"And that's the volcano. You and I are going there," he says.

"You finally tell me where I'm going, hm? Why exactly am I your prisoner again? I mean, if you wanted to kill me, you would've already done it." His mouth thins, and he adjusts a second satchel around his neck. I recognize the blue cotton of the fabric instantly. While my heart thuds and my throat tightens up, I wonder, *What's going to happen to me?*

The funicular lurches to a stop. "Shh." He ties my mouth, stares at a gold watch chained to his waist, and gulps. "Put on the cape. Let's go."

A griffin yanks a lever and watches us as a drawbridge lowers itself to the opening door of the funicular. Before Sparik sacks my head again, I notice the ornate, eagle crest around her neck and a vibrant rose cloak. She fails to hide her frown at Sparik. I keep my head low and appreciate the altitude shift. This is as close as I can get to the feeling of flying high, but I know that Kalder's altitude might as well smother me if I make the wrong move. All I can do is watch.

45

Chapter VI

"Sparik …" The voice growls like thunder flickering after the calm before the storm.

"What is your concern, O Immovable?" Sparik's voice.

"That looks too large to be a crocodile. Take off the robe. I don't need wrapping." *By Windshift's wings, he's going to* feed *me to this beast! I can't possibly be this stupid. I can't let this happen.*

Sparik chuckles. "*O Kaozar, lo Zara o lo Kaoma.* You asked me to bring you a measly crocodile?"

"We've been over this."

"Well, I've brought you a finer meal."

"This was a simple task, Sparik."

"Let's hear him speak. He had my curiosity, but now he has my attention," a new voice croons darkly.

"Prepare yourself, O Kaozar." He pauses and sighs. "And Faolani."

The new voice scoffs.

"Acknowledge him with more respect if you're going to speak with this grandiosity. I'm getting tired."

"Feast your eyes!"

He rips off my hood. I stumble on the diamond-encrusted, onyx flooring. At first, I sense nothing near me except Sparik by my side. He flaunts me and grins wildly straight ahead. I follow his gaze across the long, mammoth throne room. Then, I acknowledge the impossibility of the first deity, resting at the end of the hall, I must destroy.

Coiling around a hoard of golden coins, the beast has two graceful horns with an orb, alight with energy, between them. A fire prowls down his spine and around his angular face like a lion's mane. Slyly narrowed, his eyes are a brilliant violet. The rows of teeth are endless in his ajar mouth, and his forked tongue curls around the yellowish spears. Two large wings of yellow fire protrude from his back, but that is all. A tail, a neck, two wings, a head, and that is it. I do not bow to him.

Kaozar's eyes widen as surprise flourishes on his face. I find the owner of the new voice, sitting on an ostentatious throne next to Kaozar. A stocky, dark red dragon, with the same robe I saw from the worker who let us out into the volcano, gawks at me. His bejeweled ears (I can count seven earrings from here) prick up, and he struggles to speak.

"You got one," Faolani says, reducing me down to a number. "How?"

I take in the sheer size of Kaozar. I think fifty of me could cover his left horn. With a pang in my heart, I realize, regrettably, that he is larger than Windshift. I can understand more of his anger toward this creature now. But he can never match the pure power of the true keeper of his magic. He simply cannot.

"And, if you still need your crocodile, it's here," Sparik says, pulling the packages out of the cloth bag I saw in the cave and presenting them at the halfway point between us and Kaozar. He bows and walks back to me.

Kaozar glares at the meat, lowers his head, and picks up the packages with his lengthy tongue. Then he flings the crocodile into the air and snaps his jaws. He swallows the flesh whole without lifting his violet eyes from me. He scrunches up his nose, turns his head, and stretches his neck down to tower over me. If it weren't for his illuminated scales and mane, I would be shrouded in his shadow. "Speak."

At his demand, Sparik unbinds my snout. I cannot speak a lick of any other language other than Petrichorish—I think that is obvious—and that makes me speak what truth I have *with* what I have. "Kaozar, I am a proud wyvern. Perra Hurricane of Incus." Sparik snaps in realization and, for Kaozar, places down *my opened book in the same place he presented the meat.* He points at the pages and then to me as they converse in their own language. The god's eyes are hungry for the power in that book. *Everything Windshift trusted me with is gone.* No.

The god squints at the text and nods as Sparik perhaps translates what he is confused by. When Sparik is done, he takes the book back, and Kaozar stares into my soul. "Who are you, you tiny creature?"

"I came here in the name of Windshift." Because I have had my stealth stripped away from me, I have been left to my own deadly devices: my language and my pride.

Kaozar's confidence shatters, and he retreats to his pile. All wrinkles and fury that were there shift in the heat he exudes. "He's back." He slithers down from his coins and directly faces me. He snarls and chuckles, smoke pouring from his nostrils. I clamor backwards but keep my ground as well as I can. "You honestly think he can return to this world?"

"Y-yes." Now is my chance to show my true power.

He looks me up and down as I cover my scars. Ear-piercing laughter from him echoes through the hall. Then Faolani joins in. Sparik jumps in on the cruelty right after Faolani does.

Anger and silence burn in my veins. "You measly, misguided reprobate."

Lightning foams at my mouth. "How *dare* you?"

"I want you to know that I will never let him return," he says as Sparik notices my magic and restrains my jaw before I can fire.

Faolani lifts himself from the throne and marches to Sparik. "How? What dirty trick did you pull to get a *wyvern*?" He gets on one knee and tilts his head at me sympathetically. "Did Sparik pay you to wear this? It's a really realistic costume."

He reaches to squeeze my cheek. Electricity simmers across my scales with the narrowing of my eyes, and he yelps at the shock. He whips from me to Sparik, who flashes a smug grin. "You think this is funny, don't you? You dress up one of your little pets as a certifiable threat to our continent, you get her to *shock me–*" his voice cracks, and he clears his throat— "and you think it's some cheap joke. Your moral character is becoming weaker by the minute."

"This is not a 'cheap joke.' You're just getting offended that I'm more capable than you think. I didn't pull any dirty tricks. I got this one all on my own, relying on my acute skills. Now, ahem," he says, gesticulating to Kaozar, "can I finish speaking to Father?"

Father! He's his Father! My captor is related to a false god, the one who reduced my kind to nothing. How can a god meddle with his mortals and produce such creatures of misery to trick and strip away my power? With this brutish fury, I can pry the diamonds from the floor with ease.

Faolani looks daggers at him. He lashes his wings restlessly and returns to his throne. Large paintings of tigers and sparkling birds are endowed with geometric jewels that lounge across the walls. The only rose window I can escape from is right behind the father of the villain who fooled me.

"Now, Kaozar," Sparik says, "You've heard this wyvern's testimony. We should continue to speak in Petrichorish for her to properly understand her predicament. I found her by the southern banks of the Rojo, right off the coast near Kytrewa's walls."

What I would give for these monsters to acknowledge my existence while they speak of me. The one thing I can do is snatch my book back and feel the worn leather in my talons once more. If I only these binds around my wings could let me. Kaozar asks, a guttural snarl escaping deep from his throat, "How did she get *here*?"

"I suppose … the portal."

The god's fire licks the air from the huge oil lamps hanging from the ceiling.

Faolani paces now. "How? How could you do this to my reputation? It's me who's supposed to be–"

"Why are you taking this so hard, Faolani? I just happened to succeed. For once, you should be happy." Sparik smiles thinly. "Take a walk around the gardens, and you'll feel better from the fresh air."

"No, this cannot be happening. You are going to hide that—" he points to me— "that *thing*, and you are going to compete in the election honorably. You will not use a w-weapon of destruction to gain everyone's favor."

"Oh, cry about it."

"You won this time, Sparik. But next time, it won't be so easy. I'd be careful treading on such dangerous ground."

"Do you want me to free her on you again?" Sparik asks. It's sinking in that Sparik has forced me here to impress his brother. Is he going to use my capture to make him seem more capable to the masses? I won't be naïve. I'm not going to be an object again. *But wait. I need to bide my time so they won't think of me as a threat. Then my escape will finally be possible. My ego gets a nice boost by being called a weapon of destruction, but being docile might be my ticket out of here. If they pretend around me, I'll play their game as my own character and win it before they can notice.* While pouting, I sniffle and bow my head.

"Hmph." Faolani folds his muscular arms. "Sad. I expected something better."

Kaozar sighs. "Sons. *Please.*"

"Don't worry, Father, I'll make him quiet." Sparik says, patting me on the back.

I wail, "No, please let me go! I'm so small and scared. I'll never survive here. Whatever you do, please don't kill me. My poor broodlings will be motherless. You'd really deprive them of a mother? How could you?" This is fun.

Faolani groans and waves his hands in exhaustion. "Can it at least shoot at me or something?"

Kaozar whips his tail. When I think, with a hint of dread, that he *will* incinerate me, I silence my cries. Everyone else fixes their posture. He grumbles, "Impressive. Windshift's species isn't extinct after all these years. I'm tempted to keep you alive. So, I will. Throw her in the dungeons," Kaozar says. "If she survives that, she will face a trial in two weeks."

"No! No, you can't let that happen," I scream as guards pull me toward the exit. The vibrant colors of the room blur together, and the light from every angle turns the bedazzled guards into fireflies. I try to shoot my power at them, but they duck their heads. Whatever does hit bounces off their horned helmets, obscuring the entirety of their faces. "Let me go, you sacrilegious vermin!"

Faolani nods to Sparik. "*I'll* do it. I'll take care of 'Perra Hurricane of Incus.'"

But Sparik's expression tells a different story. I see weakness. And I feed on it, as it is the sweetest thing I have tasted in this wasteland.

"Stop! Guards, retire." He pushes Faolani out of the way and strides to me, his navy cape snapping in the air. The guards do not loosen their grip. "*I* will take this trespassing creature to the dungeons. *I'm* the one who found her."

"Oh, come *on*." Faolani stamps the ground. "Father, don't let him do this. He's embarrassing me."

"Faolani," Kaozar snaps, "quiet. Sparik has proven himself. Today, he has." He whispers, "Let him have this." The fire god then circles around the pile of gold and breathes smoke in my face. "If your god knew better, he wouldn't have let you start this imbecilic quest. What a poor, misguided soul."

Sparik ushers me outside before I can swear violence. As soon as the guards behind us close the door, Faolani roars in defeat.

I demand, "What kind of sick, twisted creatures are you?"

Sparik tightens his grasp. "You're lucky he didn't eviscerate you on the spot."

Down a balmy hallway, he shows me to a secret door away from the workers and teeming authorities. He opens the door to a long, murky, bottomless staircase. When we enter, I brace for attack, and he loses his mind.

Chapter VII

Sparik's voice cracks like an avalanche of stone. He then rips off the clamps binding my body before I can make a move. "Agh. Oh, that was difficult. Oh, I'm so sorry. I'll take off all your bondage now. I'm so sorry all this happened."

"Oh, thank Windshift, I can move."

The soft breeze whistling through the staircase is the only sound audible other than my deep breaths. The tight space beckons more heat, and I summon as much saliva as I can for hydration. Those windows must have been cracked in the hallways.

"Are you all right?" He asks.

I tackle him and bang his head against the stairs. "What in the *bowels of hell* is going on? You *drug* me, trap me, and take me to Kaozar? I'm thinking I'm going to die. I told you I didn't wanna go and see him." I squeeze and roar in his face, "But, no. No! You take me in and trick me into believing that you're some lowlife servant. And your father is Kaozar?" I scrape his cheek with my horns. "The god who wants me dead?" Before he can groan for mercy, I scrape his cheek again. "And you're going to take me to the dungeons for some ridiculous trial that might as well start with my execution to get the whole thing over with." I stop hitting his head against the stairs. Rose blood trickles from his nostrils. "You know what the worst part of all that was?"

I hear a half-hearted, disheveled, "What?" from him.

"You treated me like some sort of ticket to gain approval. I was the way you were going to impress them. I wasn't an existing creature with thoughts and feelings. I was an object. A *tool*. You disgust me. And now I'm going to annihilate you." I step back and channel my energy while easing my hoarse breath. Then I aim my head to pummel my horns into his skull.

But he scurries away from me and heaves himself up, clinging onto the brick walls. He blinks the blood from the gash in his head out of his eyes. I scoff and let him have a small respite. Once he feels safe, I can attack again. He groans but from a deeper pain than just the wounds I gave him. He says, "I want to join you."

I incredulously whip up my head. "I'm not stupid, Sparik. You can't fool me again."

"Shh, shh." The fur around his neck bristles.

"I'm not shushing."

"Then would you be a little quieter? Do you want the guards to hear you from upstairs?" He lowers his head to me and looks me up and down. "Trust me. If I let them have you, you wouldn't be breathing like how you are now. In fact, I doubt you'd be breathing at all. Can you please sit down?"

Without caring about our voice's echo through the stairwell, I say, "If you were smarter–"

He grabs the fire from the torches along the walls and lashes flames at my talons. I sit before they can touch me. "Please, listen to me. I know the last two days have been awful for you."

"Uh, *yeah*."

"But I will make it up to you."

"By Windshift's storms, will it ever get through your thick skull that I don't trust you? And I also don't have any reason to trust you at all?"

"Here's the plan. You go down into the dungeons and try to survive. At the twentieth hour each day, I will come down to you before the last chime of the hour and give you more food and water. Also, I will procure for you tomes on our history, all you need to know about Kaozaris. The twentieth hour in two weeks, I will come down and set you free. We will both get the vial, you will get *your* book– the one from Windshift– back, and we will escape." Trying to breathe, he clasps his talons to his chest. "How does that sound?"

"Oh, that's *rich*." I march down the stairs, accidentally making him scramble backwards. He whirls back and forth so that he won't miss a step as I drive him down the spiral staircase. "All the things you've put me through for the past two days could set you up for three life sentences in my world. I'm not gonna stay here for two weeks. That's insanity!"

"I'm sorry for using you, but you've seen Kaozar and Faolani for yourself. I couldn't tell you my plan before. I needed a genuine reaction from you, or else they would have known we were up to something. I didn't have a choice."

"You're *related* to them. You're trapped by yourself."

"I'm trying to be different."

At this, I crack up. It's as if I'm watching a street magician pulling ribbons and flowers out of his mouth.

"What's so funny?"

"You really think you can be different? Look, Sparik. I've met dragons like you. You try to be different, but you can't avoid everything that your father set up for you. You can't escape your privilege, you can't escape your brother, and you surely and definitely can't escape the evil that lies within you. You can sit on your throne and think you're making a difference, but you're wrong. You know absolutely nothing of what I have to do to care for my family or what I've been through."

He fidgets as if I've shown him the depths of his heart. My head takes pride in destroying his defenses, but my soul shifts uncomfortably. I tell it to stand still. "I cannot escape myself. Fine. Fine, I'll tell you. Kaozar and Giddrath regret banishing Windshift and his creations. That's why dragons like me and Faolani get elected to be entrusted with this secret: to provide a mortal view in case … he ever comes back." He gestures toward me. "And some form of him has. And I can't count the number of wars we've had on both claws. It's a blame game. But the deities know if they ever set him free, they'll experience consequences in the form of eternal pain. Worse than death. And deities cannot even die. If you and I collect the magic and set him free, we can restore peace. Finally."

I'm getting tired of this. "And how, pray tell, can I believe you?"

"Once you get down into those prisons, only then will you know the solitude of a criminal." His eyes begin to light up. "I believe Windshift is innocent."

"He is."

Guards laugh right above us. Clenching my jaw, I glare at Sparik, and he ushers me further down the stairs. Once the guards' footsteps stop, we freeze to avoid making even the smallest of sounds. After what feels like an eon, the soldiers sigh and walk back up to the entrance.

Once the door slams shut, Sparik says, "I know he's innocent. But if you see that I am lying about my plan and trying to fool you again, I'll give you what you want." He takes a dagger from his belt. Out of instinct, I shoot a lightning ball out of my mouth, which knocks the dagger clean out of his talons. The weapon slowly clangs down the stairs. "I was *going* to say for you to do your worst." I narrow my eyes in intrigue. "I mean it," he says somberly. "I've lived a somewhat happy life, knowing that peace may come to Onverra once and for all. But I can't escape myself. I cannot escape my bastard brother and despot father." He shrugs. "If I die by dagger, then my blood may revive the stone for this hallowed volcano to house and rear better creatures." He gulps as if the light from his body has snapped out of existence.

He picks up the now singed dagger and investigates what needs to be fixed in the blacksmith's den. I follow him further down the staircase.

"There will be guards down there. I'll take care of them. We may be able to get Windshift's justice," he continues, "but only if you let me help you. It's only fourteen days. You've proven to be resilient. I know you can survive until then. I'll make sure of it. The question is, do you want to?"

I consider this. His promise is everything Windshift asked of me and everything my family wants and needs.

I know nothing of Sparik. He panics like a skinny bear before winter, but he's as conniving as too many familiar faces. Yet there's a difference between creatures like Tornado and Sparik. There's no light in Tornado's eyes. In Sparik's, there is. I don't know if it's just the species, but his eyes are never dull with the brazen distaste of the world. They have the same light that Dust Devil had when he flew without a flying permit for the first time. He got in huge trouble. Father was furious. But he grinned and laughed the whole time he was grounded, locked in our bedroom. I imagine never being able to hear that laughter again. I'm honestly shocked I can still remember what it sounds like. Dust Devil wants peace. I look at Sparik who twitches and leans, heaving against the rust-colored wall. *He wants peace too*, I realize. If I look deep into my soul, I want peace. Most of all, I need allies in this world. If I'm going to hear my brother's laughter again, I'll have to take my chances. *And Sparik saved my life before he knew who I really was.*

Against all better judgment, I say, "I trust you for now. But if you don't keep your promises … " I take the dagger out of his talons and wag it in the air. "And I'll be grinning the whole time."

Sparik forces himself to nod and takes back the knife. When we reach the base of the stairs, he halts me. "Shh. Follow my lead."

Chapter VIII

"Mayi Sparik, do you need any assistance?"

"There's no need. I can transport Hurricane to her cell with ease. Ahem. You will be bones and grime before you get to see the light of day ever again," Sparik shrieks as he attempts to heave me into my cell. He grunts but tries to cover it up by uproarious and championing laughter. This false power makes him succeed. I clamp my eyes shut as I fly into the dirt, some of the ground getting in my mouth. He slides the door closed.

"You *are* going to leave me to die." My defiance is broken at the click of the lock. "Aren't you?"

Sparik starts to laugh. Then the guard laughs along. Patting the guard's back, Sparik leads him away as he slips me the satchel through the bars. Before I realize it, their footsteps echo away in the arid corridors.

I peek in the satchel and cry at the sight of the worn cover. But my heart clenches at the idea of perusing it. As I lie in the dirt, I notice the scars on my wings, legs, and tails. Too many of them are from the lava that singed me, but the ones from the crocodile sting the most. To be honest, I don't even know if that was a crocodile. Sparik told me it was, but he still lied to me. He isn't some meek servant. Of course he isn't. He's the son of a god. Windshift was right.

With horror, I open my eyes. I remembered Windshift. Oh, by his chains, I should have been praying to him this whole time! How could he have left my mind? Maybe then he could've answered my prayers from Petrichor, and I would have escaped a long time ago. What a fool I am.

I curl up and close my eyes again. "Please. Please, Windshift. Help me." I cannot obey the proper structure of prayer; only cries for help can leave my mind.

My talon becomes wet. *I thought Sparik said there wasn't any water here. Then again, he could've been lying about not only his identity but the water too.* I glance down at my unrecognizable, gray talons. A small water droplet slides down my rose and aquamarine feathers. They're dingy now and need to be preened. But why should I make myself appear more elegant? It's not worth it. I'm not worth it.

I feel another drop of water. This time it's on the ground in front of me. The liquid meets the dirt and evaporates before I can think of another sentence. I realize where the water comes from. I wipe my free-falling tears and decide to look around me.

I am able to stretch out my wings but not upward. A light on the southern wall illuminates my dark and grimy scales. A rat scampers. I can't tell where, though. The bars ahead of me are so thick and obscure that the only thing I see is one torch. Next to me is a small hole. After checking inside to see its purpose, I gag at the stench. *There's no way I can escape through that.* Other than what I assume is my bathroom, a family of spiders crawls around in the western corner, and that's it.

I list all the things I can do before this day is up. I sit. There, the list is completed. Well, I can cry and sit. I can also cry and lie down. *If Myre Gale never made me leave Cirrusmont, I would have been doing the same thing there as I am doing here. I would have moped in my house and feared what would hurt my family outside of those walls. Then again, that's a twisted fantasy. Even when I take a break from studying to walk around the hanging gardens at the university, a bolt of guilt shoots through my chest. I am disgracing my family's name.*

I decide to meet my other prison mates: the spiders. Four large ones (and at least a million babies) look quite comfortable in their home. I wish not to intrude. So, I slump back in my own corner I've designated. I lie on my back and wait for rainfall to come through the cracks. Then I remember the existence of rain here is impossible. So, I lie on my side instead.

All the time, Dust Devil and I would lie on our backs and watch the rain. Now that I think about it, this dungeon looks familiar. There isn't that pile of straw that Dust Devil had in his corner. But the cell is as dilapidated as they come. Just like me.

At least when I die, I'll be in good company.

Why am I wasting all these tears? I use them to wipe off some of the dust from my wings' talons and open the satchel, shielding the artifact inside with my wings.

The book is still there (and papayas from the island as well). I gobble the papayas, and they are the best thing I've tasted in my life.

I can't believe Sparik has given me the book back. *Why didn't he keep it? He had every opportunity to use it against me. He basically drugged me into becoming the useless sack of nothing that he dragged to the volcano. He could've used the secrets and magic in this book. That's what he wanted, right?*

To check if any of the pages are damaged, I start with the first page. The wyvern's ink is still there and so is the map for Kalder. No rips. No tears. No claw marks through any words. No shattered vial. Nothing.

No mirthless laughter leaves my soul. Oh, no! I grin and sob and hug the book until I fear its cover becoming even more loose.

I stay like this into the night. The tastes of home and papaya are sweet. Yet, they become bitter and quickly escape my tongue when the first chime of the twentieth hour down the hallway echoes against the brick walls.

Second chime. Trying to stick my head out of the bars, I peer for anyone coming down the hallway. *Too narrow.*

Third chime. There is nothing but the air becoming thicker and staler by the minute.

Fourth chime. *If only my hearing could be like my eyesight.*

Fifth chime, then nothing. I widen my eyes in order not to miss anything, the book threatening to explode from the pressure of my grip. *Nothing.* I grit my teeth together and groan. My wings cannot control themselves; they throw the book across the cell.

Labored breathing reverberates through the hall. I gasp, run to the book, and check for damage. At the sight of one of the pages being torn a little from the spine, I whine and try to put the page back together in ignorant vain.

The breathing encroaches. Spreading my wings to hide the book and satchel, I look up at the voice's owner.

Chapter IX

Sparik leans on the bars of the cell and takes deep breaths. Smoke pours out naturally. *Phew, it's just him.* As he glances down the hallway, he asks, "Still aren't dead yet, you worthless whelp?" Then he sighs and whispers, "We're fine. I came down as fast as I could."

At a loss for words, I choose the defensive so I don't stand silent like a fool. "You missed the last chime," I whisper back.

"Even though I'm the son of a god, it doesn't mean I'm perfect."

"We've known that."

"If you're going to act like this," he hisses, "I'm not going to help you. There are plenty of matters to tend to upstairs. Apologies if I've inconvenienced your luxurious stay here." Sparik tosses a piece of wrapped food back into his bag and walks away.

I bite my tongue out of the rolling pain of humility. "Sparik, I'm sorry. Come back."

I can practically hear his smug grin. He struts back and slides the meal through the bars. "I thought you'd say that. I forgive you. Also, your water and book." He leaves them to my left.

I nudge the pitcher close to me, think about whether I should wait for Sparik to leave or not, and decide on chugging the water regardless. I rub some on my scales and on my feathers as he stares. "Drinking hot lava sounds disgusting."

"It never seemed that way to us." He gives me a short bow and disappears down the hallway. "And you better stay quiet," he roars.

"Wait!" I jut my snout out between the bars and wave him back. But he continues and shuts the door behind him. I am left alone again.

Now that I have taken one step closer to hydration, I test the food. I poke the cloth wrapping, hear a rat squeak from across the room, and tear into the package before the little rodent can steal it.

Good Windshift, Sparik. You could've gotten me anything. But you get me rolled mystery meat and some flatbread. Meat! *If I've survived this long by listening to my inner compass, then I should continue.* Avoiding the meat, I nibble the edges of the flatbread. The dough gets stuck between my teeth, but my back molars can chomp down on the food and make it easier to swallow. I feed the mystery meat to the rat. Rather, I throw it across the room and expect the best. Sparik would be stupid to poison me, but I've seen what he's capable of. If there would be any time he would poison me, it would be now. *He still gave me my book back ... But it's too soon to trust him.* So, I parcel the bread in my satchel in a little pouch on the inside. Thus far the insides of the bag have been untouched by the sand and grime. That's another sign that something is going right. I'd prefer for everything to go right, but here we are.

On day four, the rat stops squeaking. My worst fear has become realized. I find myself scurrying around the room like the rat, looking for my cellmate in the nooks and crannies with light from the torches. I need my rat; the books have been perused hundreds of times. Maybe something within tells me to act like the animal I'm hunting. Then I mentally edit my sentence and say, instead of *hunting*, I'm searching. Even though I'm looking to see if it's dead, my search is not born out of malicious reasons. Then again, I did feed it possibly poisoned meat. *Then again, I ate some of the bread, and I'm sniffing the wall like I've lost my mind.* I think I've lost my mind. *No, it's only been about six days since I left Petrichor.*

Something crawls up one of my tails, and I yelp, finding the rat itself sniffing my scales.

"Hey, little guy. Please get off my tail. Pretty please?" The last thing I want again is to be embarrassed. It's not like the fellow prisoners can hear me ravaging the room and talking to rodents. I haven't heard any prisoners, actually, in these four days. *Are there any?*

"Hello?" I clear my throat. "Anyone?"

All I hear is my voice ringing through the air. I don't think I'm in the dungeons. I think I'm in a mausoleum.

Chapter X

"What'd you think about the book I gave you yesterday?" Sparik asks.

"I know it so well I can take a fifty-page exam on it. Now, give me food."

Sparik stands in front of me with arms akimbo. I try to imitate him, but having wings as what this species calls "arms" is frustrating. Trying to balance, I fall over instead.

Another tome the width of my horns is slid past the bars. He hands me a parcel of seaweed and another pitcher of water, pearls encrusted around the rim. I drink the water regardless of the pointless fanciness of the pitcher's design. Honestly, I'd take a rusty bucket over it, but I'd take either over no water at all. I'm still put off by the fact he commits to his little story about him giving me the books and somehow leading to me trusting him. My guess is that he forgets tomorrow and leaves me to rot here. *But he hasn't done that the past eight days, and he gave me seven of his own books. The most important thing is that he gave me* my *book back.*

"Now, I must be heading upstairs." He glances at his watch. "I'll see you tomorrow."

"Wait, Sparik," I say.

"What do you need? Anything?"

At this point, I didn't really realize what I wanted to talk to him about. With a shudder, I realize what I truly want: company. "When I told you that I would prefer not to eat any meat, I didn't know if you'd actually listen to me. Thank you for understanding my, uh, dietary … um–"

"Anytime. I need you alive, after all." He turns down the hallway.

"Also." He pauses. I ask, "How come you haven't tipped anyone off about me? And why aren't there any other prisoners?"

"I specifically chose this level of the dungeons because of its low security, meaning that less important prisoners are kept here, not that we have less guards." I scoff. "At the present, no one is incarcerated on this level but you. And I placed you here on purpose. No one will expect your importance if you're registered here. In our system, you're just a miscreant griffin who tried stealing an egg from the nursery. And to respond to your first question, at the risk of sounding overdramatic, you're sort of the one thing that can save our world."

"That's what Windshift told me."

His voice becomes hoarse as he leans into the border separating us, his talons wringing around the metal. "I trust him as much as you do. In order to stop the wars you read about, we need the wrongs to be rectified. Your words speak incredible volumes as a wyvern. And if there's anything *I* was born for, I believe it is this." The intensity in his eyes blooms as he walks away, tracing the one-thousand-seven-hundred-and-twenty-third brick with one talon.

The fire within me wants to learn about war. Grabbing book one again, I expect to rip through it like I've done in the past few days. While not consistent, their translations have helped. Yet those little, incomprehensible symbols in Kaozari glare back. *I got too cocky. It's my own fault for thinking I could understand every word.* When I slam the book down and flop on my back, I take book two out of curiosity. Same issue.

If Sparik really cared and wanted to help me get the vials, he would've translated *all* this for me. *He looked busy. Plus, those pestering dragons up there would've held him back. Why am I defending my captor?*

I need to remind myself that I'm in danger and can't trust anyone just yet. So, taking the book I *can* read is the best option. The pages have become warm from the insidious touch of Kalder's heat, but the disheveled book of Windshift is safe, homely.

Other than mine and Sparik's, I can't think of any other voices to comfort me. Windshift's thunder has become a blur. How am I going to remember?

I lose my page. "Great," I say, groaning. "Lovely." Flipping through the pages, the paper flutters between my feathers. Then, it lands on the inside cover. Written in luxurious penmanship is a note from the last dragon I would expect.

"Hurricane. Words cannot describe how quick this transition must have been for you. Our conversation was enlightening, and your enthusiasm was and is inspiring and enthralling. I hope that you can find this note as comfort during your travels. Turn to this page whenever you need knowledge that you are doing the greatest service that no wyvern could ever do. There is danger in Onverra as they call their world that disgracefully excludes ours. Take a deep breath. The whole continent is wishing you well, most of all me. Trust no one. You will bring me greatness. Signed, Windshift."

No ominous fire grows in my chest but rather the vehemence of my success. *I'm not dead yet! I'm close, but I'm breathing! Whatever happens, I cannot give up. I can get out alive.*

There is a problem. Windshift says for me to trust no one, but I am directly going against his wishes as I speak. What kind of follower does that? What kind of *savior* does that? While on my crusade for my god, I am going against his own will. The room becomes darker with the moving sun hiding behind the clouds. A shadow casts itself over me as if to hide my shame.

To prevent myself from going into a spiral, I concoct a plan. I'm no blasphemer. I'm simply working with what I got. I have these seven detailed albeit foreign books that I can read and were willingly given to me (without my initial say so) by the enemy. I also have Windshift's book. I can use both.

I smirk. This time, if Sparik has something under his scales, I'll be waiting.

I dive into book three in the stack. I've chosen the indecipherable, uninteresting tomes as pillows. At the bottom of the epigraph, a little note with indulgent penmanship reads the following.

"Hurricane, I can't translate this in time. So I wrote the Kaozari alphabet so you can translate it yourself. You're intelligent. I'll be back. Sincerely, Sparik."

He helps and complicates yet again.

Chapter XI

At this point, I've memorized Sparik's footsteps. On the twelfth day, though, they belong to someone else. *And there's more than one set.*

These footsteps are soft and scrape on the ground. The fluttering and gracefulness of the tiptoeing make me curious. *No kind of Kaozari could walk like that.*

But what lies out there? I have no reason *not* to look outside my cell. I just want to know what I'm up against. There's nothing wrong with that. So, as quietly as I can, I angle my head behind the bars to peer around them as my unclean fur gets in my eyes.

In the light of the torches, a griffin rests two cells down, her wings folded.

Who is this? She doesn't have any armor. Should I call for Sparik?

"*Attreka,*" she murmurs, holding out her paw to the large orange cat by her side. She lets go of the harness handle and places the leash under her back paws. The beast sits. While pulling her translucent, pink scarf tighter around her neck, she casts her gaze downward at whatever lies beyond in the cell. The long, black satin garments flicker around her russet feathered body. Grabbing for something obstructed from my view, she scratches the head of the cat that purrs at her touch. It looks like a mountain lion with harsh, gray scars around its back and face. The griffin gingerly pulls out a bouquet of wheat and rests it in front of the cell.

Why is the cat wearing a harness around its body? She's keeping the leash under her foot too. "Who is she?" I find myself asking out loud.

The cat's eyes drift away from her and toward my noise. Its pupils slit, and its tufted ears prick up.

"*Raea, oko voze?*" Her cadence does not soothe her beast. I don't think it even heard her.

The leash stays under her foot, but it extends to let the cat slink toward my cell, sniffing through the bars. I jump back. The one thing I never had to worry about back in Petrichor was getting attacked by big cats. Rarely did I ever hunt in the swamps of Tonat, so I wouldn't run into them too often.

But this one is only sniffing. Sure, its teeth are as sharp as daggers. But that doesn't mean it will kill me.

My lack of experience makes this not the most favorable. I've seen worse. I've been betrayed, so an animal potentially filled with pure bloodlust does not faze me. It just makes my throat close up.

"*Raea?*" The griffin trails along the bars and holds onto the leash with another claw. Then, after she stoops down for the harness handle too, the cat nudges the stranger toward me.

Her gaze scans the cell. *Why can't she find me?* Then, she stops at a spot next to me. Now I can get a closer look at her. Pale, featherless splotches surround her periwinkle eyes.

She says something to me. She says something … to *me.* Great, she definitely knows I'm here now, no thanks to her creature.

"Hello. Why are you down here?" I ask, taking a few steps forward. "Can you understand me?"

Her cloudy eyes meet me, and a slight frown turns down her charcoal gray beak. But the cat moves its fluffy, white paw in between the bars. I'm frozen. Its sheathed claws reach for my chest. *If it didn't hurt me before, it won't hurt me now.* I shuffle forward and let it place the pink paw pads on my outstretched wings' talons. The griffin senses the movements through the harness, and her expression softens. So does mine. Other than Sparik, the cat's eyes are the only compassionate thing to understand me. In fact, the paws are the only thing to touch me in weeks. *Its white fur is just as comforting as Baa's. How ironic that he could take the form of a predator to tell me I'm not alone.* The griffin bows and whispers something to me.

I have to blink several times for my brain to register this exchange. Then I find myself leaning forward to watch her being guided away by the cat, her dress floating in the air like a ghost.

Chapter XII

Sparik's navy cape kisses the air as he strides down the hallway. I search in his talons and find more bread and fruit, a pitcher of water, and one last book. He lets out a long sigh, heaves them through the bars, and leans against the wall.

With the fur around his neck ruffled, he closes his blue and gold eyes and freezes. I chug the water. According to the twelfth book I've been reading, he might be concerned with the Ameri—Saeri borders and his brother having Protectionist policies opposing his Unification policies. I'm proud I can remember all of that. But what else can I do while being locked in here? I savor on my tongue the last drop of water, which slips down the healed wound Tornado left me.

"Now. *Now* do you trust me?" Sparik widens his arms and paces in front of my cell. "Please tell me I didn't commit this long for nothing. I've worked upstairs, had to leave meetings and my mother and Kaozar who both have no idea I'm helping you and, if *Kaozar* found out, would have both our heads on a spike, and … Ugh, I need a breather. Okay, what I did, it was awful. And I'm so, so sorry. You didn't deserve that, and I let my pride go into overdrive. Please forgive me. Trust me this time. I will make it up to you. I will help you through every step of this whole journey. I will give up my throne to save this world from dragons like my father and brother who have no idea how much greatness your kind has. After reading the books I gave you, you have some idea of the deep-rooted hate that plagues our nations." He fiddles with his pocket watch and rubs the hidden engraving on the top. "If there was peace, my mother wouldn't have been injured."

Now I see the resemblance between the griffin and him; the fur around his neck and his hooked snout make more sense now.

"What do you know?" Sparik asks. "At least you're following a good god. At least you have a father whose approval doesn't decide the trajectory of your life. If he doesn't love me, I am nothing." He hides his face in his ringed talons, his white sleeves rolled up to his elbows.

It would be callous not to comfort him. Sparik is like a wounded animal. A shadow of what the ghastly drawings told me. "Well, Sparik," I say, "my father's disapproval of my brother decides the trajectory of my family's life. That includes me. So, I can understand a fraction of what you feel, as much as it confuses me to say that, and even though my father isn't a god."

At this, he raises his head, but his talons do not leave his face. I can see one eye peeking through his bony claws. "What happened to your brother, if I may ask?"

"Well, he shared something very private before I left. My father doesn't understand and hasn't been treating him well because of it. I hope my mother is supporting him and making him feel wanted. Well, I'm here to help him. It's all for Dust Devil. And for my mother, and the good side of my father, and the rest of my kind." I rest my head on the bars, my own walls stripped down. *Is this Sparik's doing or my own?*

He leans down to meet my gaze. For once, the first thing I think of isn't summoning magic to kill him. Instead, I listen.

"I'll come back before sunbreak at the fifth hour with a way to get to the cistern. Are you sure you're ready to escape?"

With a demigod of this fortitude by my side, I might be able to steal the vials. If I'm wrong again, my walls will be easier to build and harder to break down. I've been praying to a fortress all my life, but do I want to build one around me?

Behind me lie two books: —one ancient tome of my god and volume one of the thirteen encyclopedias of the dragon that may save my god. My eyes flit between the two, the moonlight shining on both. I feel Sparik watching over me.

I take both books and turn to him. I nod. "I'll start packing."

He grins, a protective mischief sparking in his eyes. He holds up the prison keys and jingles them.

Chapter XIII

In the quiet moments before sunbreak, we are met with a dead end. All I can see are gray stones lodged within the volcanic rock wall. As I am about to sigh in desperation, Sparik holds up a talon and inspects each stone. He smiles and bumps a rock that looks darker than its brothers. With a rumble, the wall shakes and tilts toward us. I hop out of the way. But then Sparik pulls me through the new entrance as the wall stops rotating and stays still as if it had been that way all along. A rocky pathway meets us behind that hidden entrance, spiderwebs peeking from the corners. Per his instructions, I tiptoe down it. At the end, he takes a deep breath, lets it out, and opens the side door to the cistern.

The terracotta pillars descend from the vaulted ceiling like sunbeams as sizzling, bottomless lava surrounds them. Decorated with statues of Kaozari dragons with their claws up and wings wide, the middle of the gaudy, golden brick podium is empty.

First, Sparik blinks emphatically, then his mouth falls open. "That's strange. Wait … "

"You said the vial would be here. Where is it?" My throat is closing up, so I clear it, rendering a clap of thunder to shake against the ground.

The dust settles. His voice hushes to convince me to prevent mine from echoing more. "It should be. There's no way."

"First you pushed back the time you were going to set me free. I wasn't even sure if you were coming. And now–" The sloshing of lava disturbs the tense air. We both freeze and look up at a Kaozari dragoness in the distance on a glittering bamboo paddle board. He hides me by extending his wings. I peek below his coarse wing membrane and open my hood to spy on the exchange.

"Mayi Sparik," she calls out like a spirit shrouded in mist.

"*Haz,*" he says, nodding.

She lifts from her glowing bag the vial with gold and orange liquid shimmering in the glass. My talons widen at the thought of obtaining that magic. In her language, she converses with Sparik while drifting gracefully over to the podium where she places the vial in the middle, where it suspends in midair. She bows and drifts away into the distance. Sparik shuffles away from me and hyperventilates.

"Oh, I can't believe I'm gonna do this. I can't do this. Kaozar'll know."

"Hold on. Why wasn't the vial *there*, though? In the middle of the podium before."

"Oh, that dragoness's job is to clean and check the level of the liquid. This room will open up in thirty minutes. We'll know it's that time by that window. It'll shine red with the changing of the guards outside at the sixth hour." He points. A large stained-glass window rests on the other end of the cistern, depicting the same art of Kaozar from the sketches but with a more peaceful expression.

"The bamboo paddle boards the guards use to visit the vial are *all* the way over there by the main entrance." He points to the other side of the cistern where the dragoness went. Then he pauses, glances at me, and looks me up and down. "How heavy are you?"

I shrug. "You should know. You carried me from the bank of the Rojo to the cave. The weight of two mountain lions."

"I didn't carry you over my *head*. We don't have mountain lions here."

"Well, I saw a big cat in the dungeons. You can use that as a comparison."

He narrows his eyes. "Huh?"

"I think I saw someone who looks a lot like you with her pet cat. Could be a relative."

"That was Harçia and her guide tiger. Wait. *Was* she a griffin?" I nod. "What was she doing?"

"She placed some wheat in front of one of the cells. You said there wasn't anyone down there with me, though. Why was she doing that?"

He bites the inside of his cheek and looks away. "The more time I take to explain things, the sooner the guards start to change shifts. We need to take the vial now, and I'll explain everything later." He pulls up his pant legs and steps one foot into the lava. "It's about three feet deep." Sparik wades through the lava and contemplates. Worry floods his expression as he looks at his talons then back to the podium.

I glance at the door and wipe the sweat off my face with the edge of my cloak. "Are you alright?"

He hesitates and walks back to the platform I'm standing on. "I have an idea."

"I thought I heard someone outside. You're right. We need to go. Why did you ask me how much I weigh?"

"Well, we both need to go over there. *I* will carry you, and get the vial. You just have to stay still."

"You're actually going to carry me again?"

He tucks his cape into his waistband, then he lifts me up. I shriek out of instinct but am instantly hushed with a squeeze of his talons.

"Why can't I just … fly?"

"You see that aura around the podium?" I notice a shimmer unlike anything else in the cistern around the vial's location. "Only authorized users can go through that field, including me and the griffin who cleaned the vial. If you're touching me, you can make it through." He chuckles. "I suppose this is the most flying you'll have to do for now."

Every step he takes through the lava, I feel Kaozar's power closer and closer to me, slithering into my talons and filling my lungs with air. *I wish that Windshift were here.*

He stops after trudging through the orange death in front of the podium. "I can reach here. Hold on," Sparik says, his talons on my wings as if I am a baby bird that must be protected at all costs.

"Go ahead. Quick."

As Sparik balances me with one claw, I stare at the vial between the reverent statues. *There is a vial to see, and it is right in front of me. After all this time.*

Gong! The morning bells chime. *Is it the sixth hour already? It can't be!* I whip my head around, expecting the guards to ambush us.

Sparik looks up and tries to brace himself. He places a foot behind him, but his grip still lessens. He returns both claws to my body and groans. "I can't do it. Quick, grab it." He stumbles again.

"*Me*? Me, grab it?"

"Yes, you grab it!"

Enticing me, the vial shines between the golden figures.

Gong!

I try to game the distance between the statues. Can my head fit? My talons are too thick to grab something that fragile.

Gong!

"Hurry."

Hurri? "What?"

"Quickly! I mean quickly!"

"*Oh,* right, right."

Gong!

I can't do it.

Gong–

I grab the vial and move it back to my molars instead of my canines. One more ounce of pressure applied to this vial, and I will become the bane of the lives of millions.

At the sound of clinking glass between my jaws, he runs back to the dry floor. After setting me down, he gingerly places the vial in the haversack around his neck as he fights back tears.

"T—the book," I say. "Quick, pour it on there. The book's in my bag."

"We don't have time."

I tighten my muscles. Every bit of energy surges underneath my scales. I am here.

The door opens, and I shudder. We both look to see a battalion, their faces hidden in spiked helmets. They look behind us and notice the absence of the vial, and their eyes glow with ire.

"*Hufaçi vedsza!*"

The one in the front blows a harsh tone into a ram's horn, which prompts a flurry of alerts. Then he lunges for us. Trusting Sparik to get me out of this will be difficult, but I cannot do much else now except avoid that guard.

"Fly," he says, holding onto my shoulders, the tension rising in his cracking voice. "To the window."

We nod at each other, and I fly faster than I've ever flown before.

Luckily, my wingspan fits between the columns most of the time, and other times I dip vertically, horizontally, and eventually grit my teeth together to stop screaming. I am too close. This cannot be the end. I cannot fall to a *guard*.

Sparik struggles to draw a rune in the air but succeeds to knock the mass of the guards with the light that glares from the magic symbol. Summoning glowing sunset fire, both Sparik and the general blast each other with swirling light.

The coast of the other side of the cistern appears. I let out a heavy sigh of relief.

"Sparik, let's go!"

He still struggles to shoot back. *They don't know me. They don't know my power. I know what I have to do now.* I turn around, hover midair, and gnash my teeth, launching lightning into the slits between their armor. They flail miserably and plop into the lava.

Sparik flies around me and feels around the rocks below the window. Praying that there will be another secret passage, I notice the general barreling toward me, his cutlass angled to my throat. Without a look back, I bolt toward Sparik as he opens the panel. We slide in, and Sparik slams the panel shut in the general's face. *Click.*

Chapter XIV

We rest our backs on the wall and catch our breath. In the daybreak, I can recognize white flowers snaking around the gazebos.

"Are we safe here?" I ask between breaths.

"Yes." He dusts off the ash from his shoulders and groans at the wrinkled appearance of his shirt. "The guards wouldn't crash through the stained-glass window so graciously made for *their* god. Also, only dragons in *my* family know what stone to press to open up that passage. I don't think anyone will look in the gardens. But they're going to wonder where we are. And the guards saw us, and you said my name. So they definitely know that I helped you– o-or rather us– take the vial."

I didn't think of that. "I'm sorry."

"It's fine. It's too late now. My involvement would've come out in the news sooner or later. I'm glad I can adjust to the fact I'm a fugitive now." He clasps his talons together and looks at my satchel. "Now, the book."

The alarm blares inside the volcano. "Let's find an alcove where we're more obscured," he says.

I follow him through the twists and turns of the green hedges. Squirrels with thick brown manes in the towering willow trees twitch their heads at the sound of dragon footsteps. It must be too early for them. I try to tread softly. They're too cute to be minions of an evil god.

An obsidian fountain has a statue of … *Sparik* … with the lava spurting out of his mouth into the pool surrounding him.

I look where the statue gazes, which leads us into an alcove, bedazzled with pearls.

I put on a serious face and gracefully place the book on the cobblestone in front of me. I try to stifle my laughter but in vain.

"What's so funny—Oh, the fountain."

"Your face." My snickering is the only noise other than the lava spattering out of the statue's mouth into the pool and of course the blaring alarm. "It's so … Did you *commission* an artisan to create such a *beautiful* piece of garden art?"

Obsidian Sparik elegantly postures his talons in the air and has solemnly closed eyes. His wings arch behind him in a protective pose, and the lava laps around his thin tail wrapped around the base of the fountain. Overall, he is everything Sparik has proven himself not to be.

The real, flesh-and-bone Sparik sticks his head in front of me with a pout. "Oh, stop looking at it." I laugh again. "Just wait until you see Faolani's. Each prince and son of Kaozar has a fountain. Mine just happens to be one of the newest because I'm in the running, and I happen to be alive." He shudders. "You're glad that I didn't inadvertently show you the room where the statues of his deceased sons go."

"How do they die? Aren't they immortal if they're directly from Kaozar himself?"

"Not quite. All the power is in him and the vial. He would never have all of the magic in that one vial, *but* there is definitely enough for Windshift's chains to break. Speaking of, we should get going." He fishes for the vial and shelters it in his pale palms. The orange glow around his talons glistens in my eyes.

With his eyes sparkling with wonder, he inspects and turns the vial around in his claws. The liquid slinks around like honey or molasses. But it's everything but sweet.

Then, he blinks out of his trance and delicately flips open a page. "Try the one with the fire emblem in the corner," I say. He does so, prying out the stopper, and pours two drops onto the book. Nothing happens.

Fear thickens in my veins. "Was there not enough magic?"

"I won't lie. I've never seen a book like this before. I've heard of it, but I've never seen it, touched it, been around its presence."

Then the magic beams in front of us. The crackle of the fire sounds through the air along with a clap of light. After, there is darkness. The book is found closed.

Sparik covers his mouth with his claws. "What was that?"

"That didn't happen before when Windshift gave me his magic to put in."

"Should we check the book?"

"I don't want to find out if it didn't work."

"There's only one way to know." He slides back, folding his wings closer to his body and bowing his head. "You do the honors."

I reach, my feathers becoming hotter, and open the tome. The warmth spreads to my face as I grin.

The sketches of the Kaozaris are there. The maps, the lands, everything is here. There's one problem, though. These sketches look nothing like the ones I was trained by Windshift to understand. The dragons on *these pages* look like the ones

I've dealt with prior to my imprisonment: more civilized and less unhinged.

Sparik notices my shocked expression. "His hubris is so deeply rooted into him that his magic, the pure essence of his being, paints him like a legend."

"These sketches aren't right. Well, they aren't the ones I was given by my god."

"Do you have them with you?"

"No, they're back at Castle Hill." So what if I've told him the most important location in all of wyvern history? He won't be heading there in a long time while I'm around him.

"Well, maybe he gave you outdated sketches because he's been locked in his continent for so long that he has no idea what we look like now. Sure, we looked like that before. But we evolve at the claws of our gods."

I had never thought of it like that before. That must mean that everything I've learned is wrong. Before I even consider the idea that my miseducation is not Windshift's fault, I need to know that the system that the deities thrust upon him caused this pain. Those chains, not his being, led him to my lack of true knowledge. *So, what do I have left?* I have Sparik, the Kaozari dragon Windshift told me not to trust. But he's now kept his promises. The enemy has become a little bit less of an enemy.

Yes, that's true. An enemy. But the more that I think about it, the less villainy I see from him. Everything he did had a reason supporting it. The only source of information that I get from this world is from someone else: him. I can't let that happen. I need to have my autonomy. I will coax what information I want from him. There, that's it. Then I can keep him in check. I won't leave his side. Then he can't betray me if I know his every movement. This will work, I'm sure of it.

Sparik closes the book and hands me the golden-rimmed vial. "You can set him free." He smiles with desperation lingering in the few wrinkles of his face.

"Yes … We will."

As the sound of the alarm becomes ear-piercing with the marching of soldiers beyond the alcove, the squirrels zip down the trees. Leaves spin in the air created by their quick exit from their nests. But they leave en masse and sprint in the same direction. *Something summons them.* We duck.

"Sparik, can anyone in the volcano summon squirrels? Is that a power your species has?"

"Not in my court. But I do know someone else. She's an ally. You may recognize her if I recall correctly. She can help us escape."

Confused, I turn my head, but he takes my wing and nudges me along the hedges once the army passes, against the immense, ivy-covered limestone walls.

Chapter XV

"*Mamau, oko uest*?" Sparik asks, peering through the cactus blossoms around our pathway. He mutters something to himself and continues hastily. I try to keep up but trip over myself.

Stifled sobbing rustles from beyond us. Eventually, we reach her in the middle of a small, concealed courtyard surrounded by lush desert roses and maned squirrels.

Harçia's back is toward us, her coral pink wings draped on the ground like ones of a wounded bird. Her cat arches its back around the strands of her silk dress. Harçia's head is in her claws as she shakes uncontrollably. The tiger has its head in her lap, but it can only do so much to wipe her tears.

Sparik rushes to her immediately. He hugs her tightly with his wings. He murmurs to her, and in vain I try to translate. If I can't understand words, I can understand body language. *I need to know what happened.*

Harçia's expressions are hollow. She wipes her tears with her sharp, ringed talons and hides her lion paws underneath her thighs. Then she leans over and cradles Sparik's disturbed face in her worn claws. When she does this, she reveals the emblem on her loose necklace: a series of orchids crowning a sow. Sparik pauses as she explains something, and then he holds up his talons and turns to me. "*Venai, ok'ça Hurrikaina id Petrikor.*" I clear my throat as she looks in my direction.

"This is my mother. I want her to escape with us," he says to me. "I told her you were in the dungeons."

"Why is she crying? How can she help us? Does she speak Petrichorish?" As much as I can analyze body language, the intricacies of spoken language will be forever hidden.

"No, she only knows Griffinspeak. but I can translate." he says as she absentmindedly strokes the tiger's head. "And I'm trying to ask her why she's upset, but she won't tell me. *Zoran ti, Mamau!*"

The mother pauses. "*Agiv ti teke dyçi'dia.*"

Sparik gasps with horror rotting in his throat. His language becomes unintelligible as he trips over his words. "She won't leave, Hurricane." As I slowly kneel in front of her, I look at Harçia's ethereal appearance up and down. *How much power does this Kaozar have over his creatures?* Harçia rubs the necklace, especially the emblem, as Sparik questions her. At an outburst from him, she flinches, and he tries to calm her.

I touch her knee to let her know that I care. *That reminds me of something I'd rather not remember. My family thinks I'm taking care of Tornado's concubines.* Perhaps out of recognition of my compassion, the tiger lifts its head off her lap and nudges my wing.

I hear a blip of Harçia's confession, which honestly is much less than a blip size-wise. But what I hear reveals everything. She whispers, "Faolani."

Sparik's fear and agitation vanishes in one fell swoop. It's as if a chilling breeze lurks through his fur and scales, and his expression turns to magma-filled stone. "Faolani?"

Harçia gulps and fishes in the pocket of her dress for something. She sighs and relinquishes a chiming bag in his claws. He gulps and looks at me with pleading eyes.

"Go ahead," I say, unsure of what to do myself. "Open it."

He stands unbalanced and glances inside. Shock and disgust spread onto his face like an ink blot destroying a clean sheet of paper. He takes one of the items creating the chiming and inspects a gold coin in the air.

Sparik clenches his fist over the coin and throws it on the ground. He asks Harçia one more thing, and she divulges after much hesitation. Sparik nods, folds his cape over his chest, and leans to me. "Hurricane. Come with me. We have to leave." He takes my wing and leads me down a new pathway, abandoning the griffin with the orchid necklace. I take one look back and wish that the roses' perfume soothe her beating heart.

"Sparik, what in the world is happening?"

"Faolani did something unforgivable. And we are going to leave and take this vial with us. I don't care if we have to destroy hundreds of guards. You are the only ally I have left now." He quickens his pace as the grip around the lion head of his sword threatens to chip off the gilded adornment.

Chapter XVI

The clanging of alarm bells peals through the air and disturbs my mind. *This is insane. I thought we were escaping, and now we're getting deeper into the thick of it.* I glance up and recognize the armor patterns of the patrols combing the sky. *So what if they see us? I'm probably faster than all of them combined.*

More diverse flora grows as I am pulled through the endless gardens. I've gotten so used to the cobblestone pathways that if I feel anything else at this moment, I will feel unwelcome.

Sparik rakes his claws through the bushes of orchids, roses, and vines and hacks them away from him and me. The more steps he takes through the bracken, the more warped his expression becomes. These rocks in the ground remind him of something, and that something isn't good. Yet he makes it through the thickest of the bushes and freezes in front of a sandstone courtyard. Inching back into the greenery, he immediately takes off the cobalt satchel and hands it to me.

"Whatever happens, stay behind me."

I guard both bags under my robe and peer behind him.

His cape flapping in the salty breeze, Faolani stands at the top of marble stairs in front of the sprawling, vast ocean, glittering with the rising, burning sun. His deep red scales shine from the sunbeams and the fire raging along his spine. He rolls up the sleeves of his vermillion and orange doublet, the violet buttons threatening to burst from his muscles. He looks down at us, a grin crawling onto his broad face.

"Sparik?" He has to squint to look us up and down. "The guards have spoken much of you, but I didn't believe it until now."

A growl rumbles in the back of Sparik's throat.

"What spell did she put on you?"

Sparik stares.

"I mean there's no *possible* way she got to your strong, resounding moral compass, correct?" He takes one step closer to the base of the stairs. "There's no way that you let her take advantage of you. You're too clever for that." His words drip bitter saccharine.

"Faolani, what in rotting earth have you done? What did you say to my mother?"

"Sparik, let's just go," I whisper, tugging at his cape and eyeing the pink sky beyond Faolani for any flying guards. "We have the vial."

"Hurricane, no," Sparik says. "My brother needs to answer for himself."

The massive dragon smirks. "If you wish to know, I set her free from your delusions."

"Delusions? You call wanting to save the world a delusion?"

"Oh, what *world* do you keep on referring to? Ours or theirs? What Kaozar—our *father*, mind you—has given us, or the sinful world that invaded us?"

"Why are you speaking in Petrichorish?" Sparik's voice grows. "Let's use the language of our ancestors where this knowledge won't befall on innocent ears."

Faolani is at the base of the steps now and skulks to the center of the courtyard. "Tsk, tsk. No, I don't think so. I want your prisoner to hear what I have to say about you. The truth." He quietens his voice. "You know very well what happened on the ground that you stand upon now three years ago."

The air grows blistering hot as Sparik's fire roars around his body. "Say that again." His talons seize the lion's head. I wait for him to protect me and brace for bedlam.

"I hope you know that when Harçia listened to me, she listened to the wisest thing she's heard in ages. She's going to stay here where she's safe. She'll stay here where filthy claws won't take more from her than what she already gave." Faolani hisses, "She'll be safe where you won't let those Giddrathian claws take more than just her sight again."

"May Father *damn* you!" Sparik shrieks. He brandishes his claymore and charges. The obsidian and electric blue of the blade pulse with his wrath.

I duck and hide in the hacked-away bushes. First, I need to decide whether I want to get involved in this battle. *Yes. He is my only way through this world.* So, I need to defend him. The way I aim to do that is through defending him from his brother. *Now that that's decided, how do I intervene?*

The clash of metal strikes a memory within me. The armory of Castle Hill with my battle trainer was the moment I first heard iron. I see him clearly now. The scars circled around his cheeks and neck. I sparred with him as the moon creeped along the sky.

The language of war springs up in my mind as Sparik and Faolani face off. But never had I ever imagined experiencing

Sparik's magnificent skill and the danger of choosing steel over talon.

Advance. Sparik swings his one sword to Faolani's neck with no consideration of ending his life and misses. Faolani dips behind him and pulls out two cutlasses. He tosses them into the air, catches them, and lashes his tail.

Advance again, diagonal, lunge. Faolani stabs for Sparik's exposed throat, and my ally ducks and sweeps the floor.

Parry. He follows Sparik and goes for the chest. Sparik takes his sword and fluidly deflects the point of the cutlass.

Advance. Sparik takes the cutlass in his tail and leaps over Faolani, aiming for his head. Both of them miss, but Sparik misses more. He skids along the stones.

Defense. "It was an accident!" Sparik screams in Kaozari.

"Attacking as methodically and as brutally as you did then couldn't have been just an accident. You thought you could defeat me here. I had my dragons, and you, you duplicitous snake, sacrificed your own kind for 'unity.' Even your own mother. You're not fit to rule over anything, much less by Father's throne."

They're speaking. Maybe now I can step in–

"Will you ever understand? I never thought Eirwen was going to betray me." *That's not a Kaozari name.* "We were hoping to curb your power. I had no idea she would try to destroy both of us."

"And in the process?" *Clang!*

"I got there before Eirwen took more than just Harçia's sight."

"But you got there too late. What kind of mortal would dare make such a fatal mistake?"

"No one died!" A burst of yellow magic sends Faolani back a few feet. He scoffs, outraged, and dusts off the smoke and ash from his black cape.

"One thousand, two hundred, and eighty-eight of *my* soldiers died because of you!"

"That was combined. That includes the Giddrathian forces we thwarted, but you can't focus on that, can you? I'm not going to abandon my people to have you take over."

"Then why are you trying to leave?"

Much to my chagrin, Sparik pauses. He wipes the sweat from his forehead. The alarm bells blare more loudly now in quicker succession.

"Those sirens were the same ones from three years ago." *Did Eirwen try to steal the vial too*? "Stop being a fool. We need to keep Kaozar's power within *us*. Harçia accepted it. Why can't you?" He takes a step toward his brother, breathing heavily. Grunting at the rough texture of the stones, he wipes the blood from his tail's wound on them. "*They* should be my enemy, not you. Surrvesians, *Giddrathians*." His burning gaze does the one thing I wished for it not to do; it floats down to me. "And especially you," he says, sneering.

Then he takes the claymore, snatches Sparik by the wings, and presses the blade to his throat. With his tail, Faolani puts both his cutlasses back in their sheaths.

I dash out of the bushes. "Faolani, no!"

"Hm. You haven't flown away yet. Do you want him alive?"

"YES. Don't hurt him."

"Then don't move a muscle."

The storm brews in my heart, yet I follow his orders.

"Good. Now, give me the vial."

"Don't do it, Hurricane. Don't listen to him. You can escape. I believe in you."

Gripping Sparik's wings with his claws, Faolani pricks his throat with the other. Sparik winces, shifting from his brother to me. "You want him alive," he says with sangfroid. "You don't want me to get a hold on you. If you want a chance of survival, then place your bags down at my feet."

I try to look at Sparik, desperate for a plan. Sparik gives nothing but wide eyes and an unchained fire. "I can't do it," I say.

Faolani nods and fraps Sparik in the jaw with the hilt of the cutlass. Sparik groans and reels, trying to flee from his brother's grasp. "D-do what he says."

I don't want to see the meat of a dragon, even if it is of my sworn enemy. He is just another kind in this world. Sparik is *included. His life*, I realize, *is more important than these two vials.*

The roar of Windshift's gale pummels my ears as punishment. *But what I said is true*. I can save the world, and I can save Sparik too.

Every bone in my body screams when I take the bag. Pricks of agony run through my veins as I relinquish both of my prized possessions.

I should've known. The one mere light I had in my miserable existence here would be extinguished just like that.

All those books are for naught. I never got to know how to heal.

Faolani glances down at the artifacts. "Good. Now, you wait there, and if I see you trying to escape, it's over for both of you. Now, we just wait for the guards to find and take you."

Gritting my teeth in shame, I bow my head.

"You found an obedient one." He does not let go of the claymore. "Just as obedient as Harçia. She would be so disappointed in you if she found out you took the vial. Just know she'll be where she belongs, safe with the rest of Kaozar's wives. Maybe there they'll produce a better son for him. It's a great duty for them, isn't it."

The shattering gale of Windshift, billowing through my lungs and heart again, tells me to turn and tense.

He harrumphs and murmurs something that he should have been louder about. If he was, then I couldn't have been furious about him hiding behind his quiet tone. "That's all those birds are good for." He chuckles, loosening the grip of his claymore.

Overcast and Tornado's voices mold into those cursed words. One of the many reasons I came here is to never hear language like that again. I need justice, and Sparik is overdue freedom.

"Let go of him, Faolani."

He grips the sword tighter and raises it to smite, the blade sparkling ominously in the rays.

"Wait." This time, Sparik speaks.

His brother groans. "*What?*"

"You can't kill me. If we weren't against each other naturally, we would love each other. Like the brothers we should be. But Father … he is putting us against each other. He channeled the cosmos to have our claws to each other's throats. This is a game to him just so he'll have either you or me do the dirty work of ruling Kalder, and he won't have to be the god he should be. You can't stand for this. You know in your heart that what you are doing is wrong. Y-you can help us. You can help find the vials and bring peace. You know as much about Windshift and his power as me. You're not stupid, Faolani. You're anything but. Please, drop the claymore. Let us go," he pleads, the rose-hued blood seeping into his white shirt from his jaw wound. "Would your followers want this? Would they really want me … your brother … to die?"

Faolani pauses. He opens and closes his mouth as if trying to find a response. He contemplates. *Maybe Sparik's words are working.*

"Yes. Yes, they would." He aims to strike.

In a clap of turquoise, I summon a group of lightning bolts to his chest. My power knocks him down, and Sparik regains his strength. He grabs his claymore and slices Faolani's leg and wing.

"C'mon, Hurricane. Let's go!" I snatch the haversacks and clamor up the stairs. Sparik leaps into the air and starts to fly. Seeing these creatures in flight is like seeing a raven blacken the air. Now that the sun has risen, light returns.

Faolani drags himself up the stairs like a rabid beast. I screech and claw him with my talons, creating a deeper gash in his legs. He snarls as his blood pools onto his ornate, white pants, and he glowers and retreats to the wall surrounding the top of the staircase. I glance down and feel the comfort of altitude as water slams into the basalt cliffs below me. *Perfect.*

I dip down to the waves, twirl the seawater in the air, and blast him in the face. The water singes his maw, melting off the scales and creeping into his left eye. Without turning back, I join Sparik in the clouds with all my might as Faolani's agonized screams are deafened by the alarm bells.

Chapter XVII

Mountain lions pick the weakest prey to chase, bite, and tear. The leader is the most powerful, but in Petrichor, it's the one who gets the first cut.

The air roars in my ears with the tension of the chase. Blood from my ear spreads to my cheek and neck as I swerve through the arrows shot by the sentinels of the volcano. I've been prey for too long. It's time I fly.

Sparik, on the other talon, struggles. His coarse breath interrupts my focus. "They're going to start firing magic soon."

"How bad does it get?"

We find out immediately when a giant fireball narrowly escapes the top of my head. The blaze slams into the ocean and fizzles away. Soon, at least three hundred of them rocket near us. All I can see is smoke, but the smell of fear is stronger.

I look behind me to see where they are firing. From the cliffs and sentinel towers, guards with the same, morphing black armor from the cistern hurriedly and systematically draw runes in the air. The golden magic glows in place then snaps and crackles as it forms into aggressive blazes. The guard casts them at us, and the process starts again.

"Duck!"

I can't tell whether the command is from him or me, but we both follow it. They come from all angles. At this point, I wait for the guards to come for us in the flesh. I look back again.

Nothing. They stay firm on the cliffs and continue their assault.

Above them, a crack in the volcanic rock rumbles through the sky.

"Oh, no. Oh, no, no!" Sparik yells. "He's coming."

"Who?" Then I think of the one male creature strong enough to cause that break in the rock. Then, my suspicion is deemed correct.

First, smoke swells out of the vent. Sparks shoot out of the nostrils of the beast. Then, the head snakes through the top. The orange veins pulse violently through dark scales as he slithers, thunderingly slowly, around the volcano like an anaconda suffocating his game. His mammoth size makes the volcano itself pale in comparison. He is a red stain on the sky. The yellow orb between his horns is like a teardrop from the sun. His mouth is a large, dark ravine plastered on his face like a scar of something meant to be forgotten.

The monolith of Kaozar himself.

"Cease fire," he bellows. The guards shift and bow, draping their wings across the ground and overlapping each other. Their bows and arrows clatter on the raw granite.

A tsunami of dust closes in on us, provoked by his sheer strength. Sparik and I shut our eyes before the rock and grime pelt our scales. The wave calms down, merging with the water below us. Now we can see Kaozar in his potency.

"Sparik," he grumbles. His eyes flit downward. Crowds of peasants from the docks and in the volcano swarm to cheer and roar at his arrival. Viscerally, they cry.

Fueled by his creations' praises, he puffs out his chest and dips his head, baring his teeth. "What have you *DONE*?"

Silence penetrates all of our hearts after the howl. I swim in the quiet, gasping for air from the still-settling dust. Sparik's expression chills. I try to talk to him, try to get him to speak. But his fire seethes on and on.

A myriad of debris floats up to the disturbance of the volcano's vent, but one of them has wings. I peer while desperately trying to keep afloat in the air.

I know that black cape with the burning pink sun insignia well. Sinking his talons into the rock, Faolani stands on the edge of the vent. He folds his wings behind him along with his arms. I believe he is disheveled but intact. Even from here, I can sense his outrage over our victory.

But then I see every minute detail of his scar. The boiling flesh simmers from the top of his forehead down over his left eye. Then it pivots and curls around his snout, seeping into his jaw. The exposed muscle throbs from the torn scales. Even though my heart burns at the fact he still stands well, part of my soul convulses at the sight, and the other part is glad my sense of smell is not strong enough to detect the roast. *Was that ... from just water?*

"Return from whence you came, Sparik," the unmoving god says. "I command you."

Sparik is silent.

Faolani decides to speak, throwing up his arms. "Do you see what she did to me, Father?" Shuddering, he struggles to point to his scar. "I'm disgusting! We cannot let him and his wretch escape. I look like a monster!"

"Faolani, be quiet." Kaozar judges us from afar. The sun illuminates all of his features even though the rest of his body is concealed inside the volcano. I imagine all of its floors crashing down on the bottom level from the dragon hearing the news of the loss of the vial and his disobedient son. "Sparik. If you do not return, there will be consequences." I still do not bow.

Deep in his soul, something awakens. Sparik gains composure, and his words rampage through the heat. "I will not return. I will save this world by her side–" he nods to me– "and all these never-ending wars will finally end. And if I must relinquish my position from the throne, then it'll be a small price to pay."

"It's unfortunate you say that. You had potential, dear son of mine."

"I'm no dear son of yours. I'm nothing but a burden to you." The waves crash on the shore asynchronous with our wingbeats. "But with Perra Hurricane of Incus's help, I can be something more. Now, let us go in peace." He begins to turn and beckons me to follow.

"We'll let you leave. But know that when you leave, you can never come back."

Sparik pauses, the demigod's back to his father. After a long period of painful silence and contemplation from him, he nods in peace. My eyes widen. *Will Sparik leave his throne ... for me? Is my existence that momentous?*

"I see." Kaozar clears his throat, the sun shifting its location in the sky at the sound. The crowd is on tenterhooks for their god's next word. "Faolani?"

Sparik bristles.

Kaozar grins, his teeth like white mountains. "I'm pleased to announce that you, my son, have succeeded in the election. You are now my Advisor and the ruler and voice for the mortals."

The pain from the wound disappears. He stands tall, and Faolani's expression dawns with pure joy.

Sparik clenches his teeth and breathes heavily. "Father, no. No, you can't."

"*Silence, Sparik!*" The force of the god's voice brings us closer to the water. Each wave towers over the next. "You made this decision. If my creations find you or your wyvern on our territory, your heads will be on a spike, and your bodies will be melted at the bottom of the ocean."

Tears waterfall down Sparik's face. Now I notice his wingbeats are less strong. I don't know how long he'll be in the air. "*Mamau! Za lenu gittrak!*"

For him, I search the crowd chanting Faolani's name. Harçia is among them, but there is no glee in her voice. She and her tiger stare at the horizon behind us. Her eyes try to guess where we are. *There is still hope for her.*

Faolani basks in the applause. He laughs in triumph as he floats down to the base of the volcano above the hoi polloi. He spreads his black, tattered wings and coughs up blood.

"All of my dear followers. We have won the battle today. But we will have to work together to win the war. My brother has decided to betray us by running to the enemy, the Giddrathians. What do we say to that?"

Sparik's world shatters at the resounding decries.

"We say no. We say we protect the Kaozari species from outliers. Our domain is our domain. What do we say to the Giddrathians?"

They scream for their blood.

"I see I have taught you well. You see what his wench has done to my face?" At the second time he's acknowledged the gash, the crowd cries. "Exactly. I cannot be weakened as your leader by the evil magic and nature of the other continents. All we can trust is ourselves." He raises his fist in the air. "We are ourselves, or we are no one. Let us protect the Kaozari species." He sees both of us still flying. He smirks. "And crush the naysayers."

Sparik and I won't have to worry about treading back on Kaozari lands again. We have what we need. We don't need to risk our lives against corrupt talons.

"Let's go, quickly," I say. I don't get a response, so I look to my right.

Sparik is completely wan. His vision is locked on his brother's success and his father's joy. It's as if he was never there. His eyes loll, and he swallows one too many times for me not to be concerned. That concern turns into worry which turns into sheer terror.

He shuts his eyes and dips his head back. *He isn't doing this on purpose, is he?* No, he isn't. With his body limp, he plummets toward the ocean.

"Sparik!"

He gets closer and closer to the roaring whitecaps. I know that the dark blue will consume him and turn him into a heap of burning flesh.

Windshift's words find their way into my brain as I feel the sea breeze on my scales. *Trust no one*. If I started diving after this unconscious Kaozari, I would be stricken down with lightning. *No, I can't forget he's on our side. He has proven that to me countless times. If I disagree with Windshift, what will happen to me?*

But I owe him. Don't I?

Epilogue

STRATUS

"Eaaah!" I clamp my mouth shut, hoping to swallow the next yawn.

The rest of the congregation glares back at me. It's not my fault today's sermon is as boring as listening to a lecture about the genomes in snails. We're going to fall out of favor with Windshift if we do too many wrong things! We're going to die soon, and we need to be better! *Oh, get a grip.* I don't have to worry about any of this.

The sermon has ended now. All we have to do is pray. Then I can leave and stretch my legs. It's hard to be me, a fidgeting mess, among a group of completely devout wyverns. Look, Windshift has been a part of my life for a long time. I love him. He gave my family all that we have, and that's great. I'm just tired. And it's way too packed in here, and this rug is too small.

But we can get off it now. I find my way to the base of the podium and shove into a few strangers over a candle. I was dragged all this way, and so help me Windshift. I'm going to pray to that little candle and the bowl of rainwater.

I start with something easy. "O Windshift, O Unmovable. Thank you for bringing my lungs and wings air today. I pray that you help me. Help me with what?" *I should really be more formal. Oh, who am I kidding? Windshift knows who I am. If I was to act fancy, then it would be a lie.* "Please keep me well.

And, um, I've been having trouble with this chord on the lyre. My teacher says it should be easy, but my wings' talons just don't bend that way. And–"

"Please, everything hurts."

That's a new voice. I glance to my right. Dust Devil bows his head above the bowl as his tears create ripples within it. He gapes at the candle flickering in the grumbling and murmuring masses. "Please. Get me out of here. Get me out of this body, get me out of this home. This is not a home. I'm in grave danger. I can't deal with Cyclone anymore. I can't do it." He freezes, gasping quickly and quietly. Then his expression turns crooked. He glowers at the candle. "Why did you do this? Why did you make me a wyverness? I could have been a true soldier. I could have been perfect. But you." While the words of the masses are apologetic and reverent, the fire burns in his eyes only adding to his rage. "*You.* You threw me into this *prison.* You had every chance to rectify this, but you didn't. You could've changed me, but you didn't. Every day I wake up, and I live with your stupid mistake." He searches for the words and finds them as if aiming a knife to their necks. "How could you be a god if you do this?"

This makes me shut up. I stretch my wings around him and let him sob into my shoulder. My talons drudge through spreading the rainwater onto our cheeks and across our eyes. I take my drenched talons and extinguish the flame.

"Stratus?" As Hurricane's family and I leave the temple, Dust Devil appears behind me suddenly and jumps down the marble steps. "I'm sorry you had to see that."

Once Teal walks ahead of us, I console him. "Never say sorry for that."

"It's just … something is off." He sweeps away his mane from his eyes. "She said she'd be back now."

I try to picture Hurricane and don't have a hard time doing so. Whether she's alright or not is all I've been thinking about. "She specifically said that she'd be back in a few weeks."

"Two weeks constitutes a 'few weeks.' I miss her."

"I do too."

Going back to the castle is easy. The temple is on an island close to the entrance, so it's only a matter of hopping off the edge and floating down with the rest of the family. But Dust Devil gets an idea in my head. *Where* is *Hurricane*?

"I don't know where she is," Dust Devil says, somehow reading my mind. Our species cannot read minds, so I take it as some weird divine intervention.

"She said she was at that school for maids. We can't just waltz in there and talk to her."

Dust Devil pauses midair. "Why … don't we?"

I bark a laugh. "She's busy."

"Surely not busy enough to avoid us." He gives a half-hearted smirk. "Right?"

"But what about your parents?"

"They probably won't know we're gone. We just need to know where the school is."

"Dust Devil?"

"What?"

I lean close. "Hurricane told me to protect you all. It's my duty to make sure we don't get into trouble."

"Stratus?"

"Hm?"

"I appreciate your help. But we need to do something. I need help. I can't stay in the castle anymore." He narrows his eyes. "I'll take any chance I get to see my sister again."

I nod, contemplating. His parents are going to kill me. But I want to see my friend too. We glance back at Teal, and all we see are her tails slipping behind the massive gates. *She must think we're still behind her. Let's keep it that way.*

I smile. "We're going to make that happen."

After trying too long to decipher the maps having the graffiti furiously scrubbed off them by maintenance workers, we fly to where the house of the concubines is. We flash our rings on our wings' talons to the muscular guards over the birch door, and they let us into the house, their eyes following Dust Devil the most.

Violet and turquoise water dripping from the stone vents is the only sound that fills the room. At the end of the hall is a small desk. I decide to make the first move by alerting whoever is here by our presence. "Hello?" We meander down the stone pathway to the desk. A door stands imposing behind the desk, and I try to see what is inside.

Before I can, a short wyverness pops her head up. The beads wrapping around her head like a diadem sway in the air. "Why, good afternoon. Welcome to the Palace of Fertility." Dust Devil gives me a confused look but tries to suppress his feelings with a grimace. "Do you have an appointment with any of the wyvernesses?"

"Well, technically." Here it goes. "Do you have someone named Perra Hurricane of the Plains of Incus training right now to be senior maid? We're her family."

"Do you have an appointment?"

I clench my teeth. *Why can't she just give us the answer and tell us she's here?* "I unfortunately do not have an appointment, but–"

The wyverness's tone shifts radically. "Confidentiality is our top priority. No meetings with the wives until you have an appointment. Come back when you've made one." She leaves the desk, slides behind us, and struts down the hallway in the opposite way from where we came, casting us a furtive glance.

We follow her as though we are leaving, and when she closes the door behind her, we stop and sigh. "Well, that was useless," I say. "I'm sorry, DD." My snout turns up in surprise at the new nickname. I search his face for approval.

Looking at his feet, he narrows his eyes. Then his gaze drifts to the ajar door behind the desk. He tsks. "Follow me."

Oh, come on. "Dust Devil–"

"Listen to me," he says heavily. "I need this. I need to know why she hasn't come back yet. What's the worst that could happen?"

"We could get caught. And we'd get in a ridiculous amount of trouble with the Castle Hill officials. Considering Hurricane is working for him. Scratch that. Considering Hurricane was worthy of being chosen to work for him, we should act like that too. Or at least try to." Plus, his parents are going to kill me.

He looks me up and down. *How bad is my mane? I brushed it with the little shell comb that the castle gave me. It has this little diamond in the middle of it. It's so clean; I can see my reflection.* "Suit yourself." He marches behind the desk and slips inside the room.

"Dust Devil," I hiss. "Come back." Well, now I'm alone. What does it mean for me that I'm alone here? I'm not sticking my snout where it doesn't belong. But I should … Dust Devil needs help. I've seen the depths of his soul, and he shouldn't be alone right now. But if I'm not protecting him well enough, then I'll get sent home, and he'll be stuck with Cyclone. I check behind me for any workers and gulp.

"Stratus?"

My head whips up. "Yeah?"

"You're … gonna wanna see this."

My mama always told me to follow directions. Keeping the door slightly ajar, I follow him. Inside the room are piles and piles of paperwork. The small, brown wyvern sifts through the stacks of papyrus.

"H," he murmurs to himself. "H, where is *H*? I just lost it. Hold on."

A scratched clipping of some ancient tome is tacked onto the wooden board hung on the wall amongst the rest of the various advertisements. I brush aside the "Make Your Own Ram Horn, Call Your Friends" flier and inspect Tornado and his group of wives. All six of them have their faces speckled with pearls and smiles except the one closest to Tornado. She has a thick neck but is almost as tall as Tornado himself. I would describe her face if it wasn't torn off.

"Here, come on." Dust Devil nudges me on the shoulder, and I snap out of my daze. "Look." He points to the packet.

"This is where Hurricane's name and painting should be. But it's not there!"

"So …"

"Hurricane isn't here." Realization dawns on his face. "What has Windshift done to her?"

I aim to discover the answer to that question. If I can walk into this room without any consequences, what's the damage of looking back around the castle and asking around for her? It's not like I'll be making some sort of trek. I can trust Windshift. But Dust Devil's expression still pains me. I can understand how he does not trust him. I hope to help him know he is loved.

"We're going to find her," I say, patting him on the shoulder. "And we're going to get answers."

He smiles assuredly. "Also, DD is a decent nickname. I approve."

I beam.

fire mane
Ventral + dorsal are same
No... talons? or legs...?
Whale tail?
why the black marks?
sun?

ACKNOWLEDGMENTS

Another one in the books! Huzzah!

I would be remiss if I did not reiterate my thank you to my writing teachers. Each and every one of you has supported my dream to create with unfailing kindness.

Thank you to the late nights of binge-watching various media, each hour spent enriched in inspiration was worth it to make it here, even if the circles under my eyes have grown.

I was thrilled to discover my book *Petrichor* is being read all over the world, and it's thanks to The Bookwyrm Lair and the passionate people who support it. Thank you for giving me a platform to reach hundreds of readers (so far).

My gratitude grows for my online friends who have genuinely supported me since the creation of this series and when it was just an idea. Danny, thank you for your detailed thoughts regarding *Petrichor,* and I'm so glad I reached out to you after all this time.

I tip my hat to my community Writing Club. You all have great talent, and thank you for your continued encouragement.

Thank you to my dear friends—Adam, Alex, Christian, Gabe, Hutch, Jackson, and Sydney—who would listen to me if I rambled about a character problem or if I needed advice about word placement. May our student athlete grinds never quit.

To everyone who attended my first publishing party, we had
a fantastic time! To my lovely hosts, Gracie and the
velociraptor who has moved from my backyard into my
house, without you two, the whole event wouldn't have been
possible.

I give a hundred and more of my thanks to Jody Dyer, my
editor and publisher who has been incredibly patient and
thorough with me. I'm fortunate to work with her sharp wit
and wonderful talent, and I felt so proud to introduce her to
my supporters at my first book signing.

My endless gratitude to my mother and father, who have
supported me in ways I will never know. From every day of
editing, mulling over character development, and
encouragement, you have given me opportunities that I am
blessed to experience. *Thank you.*

ABOUT THE AUTHOR

C.E. Wright wants one thing out of life: joy. So she pursues it. Everything fantasy and romance, she adores. If she wants to write it, she will. She lives in suburban Nashville, Tennessee, where fried chicken runs wild in her blood. It's not as if Music City is teeming with a dragon population, but C.E. Wright nevertheless appreciates the art-cultivating atmosphere the city presents. In her spare time, she drills her Japanese and French conjugations, plays classical piano, creates art of her characters, and chugs boba tea.

Book 1 - Petrichor
Book 2 - Kalder

Coming soon ...

Book 3 - Alphi
Book 4 - Ióda
Book 5 - Maelstrom

Follow C.E. Wright here:
https://artfight.net/~c-e-wright
https://twitter.com/ce_wright8
https://www.tumblr.com/blog/c-e-wright
https://www.facebook.com/profile.php?id=100087305438084&sk=about